The Dorset Boy Book 15 – Burm

Acknowledgements

Thanks to Dawn Spears the brilliant artist who created the cover artwork and my editor Debz Hobbs-Wyatt without whom the books wouldn't be as good as they are.

My wife, who is so supportive and believes in me. Lastly, our dogs Blaez and Zeeva and cats Vaskr and Rosa who watch me act out the fight scenes and must wonder what the hell has gotten into their boss. And a special thank you to Troy who was the grandfather of Blaez in real life. He was a magnificent beast just like his grandson!

THANK YOU FOR READING!

I hope you enjoy reading this book as much as I enjoyed writing it. Reviews are so helpful to authors. I really appreciate all reviews, both positive and negative. If you want to leave one, you can do so on Amazon, through my website, or on Twitter.

www.thedorsetboy.com

About the Author

Christopher C Tubbs is a dog-loving descendent of a long line of Dorset clay miners and has chased his family tree back to the 16th century in the Isle of Purbeck. He left school at sixteen to train as an Avionics Craftsman, has been a public speaker at conferences for most of his career and was one of the founders of a successful games company back in the 1990s. Now in his sixties, he finally writes the stories he had been dreaming about for years. Thanks to inspiration from great authors like Alexander Kent, Dewey Lambdin, Patrick O'Brian, Raymond E Feist and Dudley Pope, he was finally able to put digit to keyboard. He lives in the Netherlands Antilles with his wife, two Dutch Shepherds, and two Norwegian Forest cats.

You can visit him on his website
www.thedorsetboy.com
The Dorset Boy, Facebook page.

Or tweet him @ChristopherCTu3

The Dorset Boy Series Timeline

1792 – 1795   Book 1: A Talent for Trouble.
Marty joins the navy as an assistant steward and through a
series of adventures ends up a midshipman.

1795 – 1798   Book 2: The Special Operations Flotilla.
Marty is a founder member of the Special Operations
Flotilla, learns to be a spy and passes as Lieutenant.

1799 – 1802   Book 3: Agent Provocateur.
Marty teams up with Linette to infiltrate Paris, marries
Caroline, becomes a father and fights pirates in
Madagascar.

1802 – 1804   Book 4: In Dangerous Company.
Marty and Caroline are in India helping out Arthur
Wellesley, combating French efforts to disrupt the East
India Company and French-sponsored pirates on Reunion.
James Stockley was born.

1804 – 1805   Book 5: The Tempest.
Piracy in the Caribbean, French interference, Spanish
gold and the death of Nelson. Marty makes Captain.

1806 – 1807   Book 6: Vendetta.
A favour carried out for a prince, a new ship, the SOF
move to Gibraltar, the battle of Maida, counter espionage
in Malta and a Vendetta declared and closed.

1807 – 1809   Book 7: The Trojan Horse.
Rescue of the Portuguese royal family, Battle of the
Basque Roads with Thomas Cochrane, and back to the

Indian Ocean and another conflict with the French Intelligence Service.

1809 – 1811   Book 8: La Licorne.
Marty takes on the role of Viscount Wellington's Head of Intelligence. Battle of The Lines of Torres Vedras, siege of Cadiz, skulduggery, espionage and blowing stuff up to confound the French.

1812   Book 9: Raider.
Marty is busy. From London to Paris to America and back to the Mediterranean for the battle of Salamanca. A mission to the Adriatic reveals a white-slavery racket that results in a private mission to the Caribbean to rescue his children.

1813 – 1814   Book 10: Silverthorn
Promoted to Commodore and given a viscountcy. Marty is sent to the Caribbean to be Governor of Aruba which provides the cover story he needs to fight American privateers and undermine the Spanish in South America. On his return, he escorts Napoleon into Exile on Alba.

1815 – 1816   Book 11: Exile
After 100 days in exile, Napoleon returns to France and Marty tries to hunt him down. After the battle of Waterloo Marty again escorts him into exile on St Helena. His help is requested by the governor of Ceylon against the rebels in Kandy.

1817 – 1818   Book 12: Dynasty
To Paris to stop an assassination, then the Mediterranean to further British interests in the region. Finally, to Calcutta as Military Attaché to take part in the war with

the Maratha Empire. Beth comes into her own as a spy, but James prefers the navy life.

1818 -- 1819   Book 13: Empire
The end of the third Anglo-Maratha war and the establishment of the Raj. Intrigue in India, war with the Pindaris, the foundation of Singapore, shipwreck, sea wars and storms.

1820 - 1821   Book 14: Revolution
The Ottoman Empire is starting to disintegrate. The Greeks are starting to revolt. Marty has a promise to keep so Britain can gain Cyprus. Just to complicate things King John of Portugal needs his support as well.

1822 -1824   Book 15: Burma
The 1st Anglo-Burma war is looming, and the East India Company and the British Government need an excuse to start it. Marty is sent to Burma as Ambassador to get things moving.

Contents

Orders

Gibraltar

The Winner

Storm

S o Luis

Cape Town

The Longest Leg

A Cool Reception

The Boat Race

Festival

Incident at Khote Wa

The French Envoy

Escalation

Ambush off the Andermans

Manipur

Assam

Escape

Calcutta

Narayanganj and Cachar

The Bridges

Preparing for War

Combat

Blockade

Epilogue

Historic Notes

   Glossary of sailing terms used in this book

Orders

Rear Admiral Martin Stockley, Viscount Purbeck, codename M, sat in his study and read the commissioning letter. He had been aware that his name had been progressing up the list as those above died, retired or were promoted, but it had come as a surprise when his name had risen to the top. He hadn't studied the lists or read the Navy Gazette for at least a year. He was coming up to forty-three years old and was a hugely experienced officer, agent, and diplomat.

He put the letter aside and rang a bell on his desk. Sam, his coxswain, opened the door a little too quickly to have been other than stood outside. His grin gave away that he had guessed what the letter with the fouled anchor had meant.

"You knew?"

"I reads the Gazette." Sam grinned, his white teeth shining from his ebony face.

"And you didn't remind me?"

"Aw now, Boss, don't be a grump. You deserves it."

"You have been spending too much time with my daughters. Grump indeed." Marty resisted the urge to laugh.

Two more faces appeared.

"Congratulations, Daddy," they said in unison.

"I suppose I had better go to my tailors." Marty sighed then laughed and held his arms out for a hug from the twins.

"It's a shame your mother is in Jamaica. She would have enjoyed a trip into town."

"We can come, can't we?" Constance asked.

"Please," said Edwin.

They would both be leaving as soon as their mother returned in around four weeks. Constance to Newmarket to learn about horse breeding and medicine and Edwin to Eton.

"Alright, get your coats. Sam, you come as well."

He asked one of the footmen to have the landau brought around. It was early spring, the weather was fine and riding in the open-topped carriage would be pleasant.

Adam appeared with a small trunk used to transport his dress uniforms. Marty looked at him quizzically.

"Your commodore's uniforms are almost identical to a rear admiral's. They just need adjusting to fit perfectly and the emblems changed." He was right of course the step from Commodore to Rear Admiral was a small one and, despite impending middle age, Marty still had a slim figure.

Sam loaded the trunk onto the landau and took a seat next to the driver. The twins climbed aboard followed by Marty. The driver, seeing everyone was settled, flicked the reins and the matched pair of bays stepped forward.

A week later Marty was summoned to the Foreign Office to meet George Canning, Foreign Secretary and Head of the Secret Service, who had taken over after Robert Stewart had committed suicide the year before.

"Martin, welcome. Congratulations, Rear Admiral." George said when Marty was shown into his office.

"Thank you, George, I hope I find you well?"

"In splendid health, thank you. Coffee?"

They sat in club chairs and savoured the brew silently for a moment or two. Then George sighed. "I have a job for you." Then he sipped more coffee.

Marty waited.

"You are familiar with Burma?" he asked looking up at the ceiling.

"Yes."

"The Konbaung Dynasty rules it and since the middle of the last century they have been attempting to expand their empire. They fought and beat the Chinese and forced a treaty and trade agreement on them. That gave them the resources to look west. Now they are beginning to butt up against our plans for north-eastern India. As part of that they are encouraging their freelance mariners to raid our shipping."

"You want me to take a squadron over and stop them?"

"Not exactly. We want you to be ambassador to the court in Ava."

"Ava? I thought Amarapura was the capital."

"It was but they moved it to Ava in '21. You will start a mission there."

"Oh? So, what am I to do there?"

"King Bagyidaw ascended the throne in 1819. He is a healthy thirty-eight years old. Under his rule the border between them and us has become wilder with raiding from both sides. We have requested that an ambassador be put in place to try and smooth things over, but I have very little hope that you will succeed. They are constantly at war with Siam and kicked the French out of Burma. Unfortunately, the French remain in the frame with their consolidation of French Indochina. Vietnam is right on the Burmese border."

"What do you want me to do?"

"Keep their relations with France at arm's length and foul up their relations with Siam using whatever methods you find expedient. We want to keep their attention down there."

"An open remit?"

"Yes. We will leave the decisions to you."

Marty puffed out his cheeks, this was big.

"You can select your ambassadorial staff yourself."

"And my ship?"

"I understand the Unicorn has arrived back from the Caribbean. She is all yours. The rest of the SOF is staying in the Aegean."

"How has Beth got on?"

"Famously. The Liverpool connection has been broken and the agent arrested. They sunk four of his ships and took one as a prize which has been bought in. The Fox is now part of the SOF."

"Fox? She called it the Fox?"

"Yes, is that significant?"

Marty laughed. "Beth is a study of family history is all."

George looked at him, puzzled, for a second or two then it dawned on him.

"That pirate ancestor of Caroline's! Of course, her ship was the Fox. Well, she best be comfortable on it as she will be out in the Caribbean for a while yet."

Marty was happy about that, it would give Caroline a free hand to organise the wedding. Then he too had a realisation.

"Will I have to take Caroline with me?"

"It's a three-year posting so I would if I were you."

"Three years? Oh Lord, the wedding!" Marty exclaimed.

"Wedding? Oh, you mean Beth and Sebastian? When was that due?"

"Spring next year."

"I see the difficulty. But this has to take precedence over personal issues."

"I understand, and so will Beth and Caroline. Although neither of them will like it."

"Now, about your team. Who would you like for Military Attaché? Wellington has a suggestion, which might make things easier for you on the home front."

Marty groaned inwardly, he knew what was coming and in any other circumstances he would have welcomed it.

"Major Ashley-Cooper?"

George gave him a wide smile.

"He would be ideal but—"

"Excellent," George interrupted, giving him no chance to finish the sentence.

Marty arrived home and slumped in a chair with his orders and portfolio on his lap. Adam entered the room, took one look at him and poured a large brandy.

"Thank you, Adam." Marty took the proffered glass and took a healthy swig.

"A new assignment, Sir?"

"Yes, we will be leaving as soon as my wife returns."

"May one ask?"

"One may. We are going to Burma. A three-year posting. It will be a new residence so we will be packing the house."

Adam understood why Marty looked so – strained.

"The wedding?"

"Postponed until we get back."

"Miss Beth —"

"Will have to put up with it. Sebastian has been appointed as Military Attaché."

"I will get the staff started." Adam bowed his way out as Antton came in.

"I heard."

"All your wives can come too."

"Mine can't."

Antton's love, Steffanie, was the widow of a former governor of Ceylon who died in a horse-riding accident. Her son, the heir to the family fortune, was Antton's child but that was a secret only a few knew. The couple spent as much time as they could together without the family ever seeing Antton and the child together as the resemblance would leave no doubt about who the father really was.

"Do you want to stay behind?"

"No, that is not what I want. My first priority is always the team."

"None of us are getting any younger, my friend."

"True but we are all still capable. If a little slower. How long will we be away?"

"Three years. Maybe less if things deteriorate."

"Beth is not going to be happy."

"I will write to her and tell her what has happened, but from what Canning told me she will be over there for some time. Sebastian will be with us. Canning has appointed him Military Attaché."

"He expects trouble then."

"That's why we are going and not a regular diplomat."

Caroline returned on time, full of stories about the new plantation and Beth's goings on. She was so excited to see Marty she didn't notice his slightly reserved attitude until they were halfway home. He told her about the posting. She was silent, her face neutral. He knew better than to say anything.

"Beth?" she said finally.

"I have written to her, but her mission will keep her in South America beyond the planned wedding date anyway."

"And Sebastian?"

"Has been appointed our military attaché."

"Did you?"

"No, Canning appointed him on the recommendation of Arthur."

Silence returned until they turned into Grosvenor Square.

"The house?"

"Adam and the staff are packing."

"Ship?"

"The Unicorn."

"That won't do. We will need the Pride as well."

Marty didn't reply.

"Anything else I should know?"

"I made Rear Admiral."

"About time."

Gibraltar

It took Caroline a day to come to terms with the news after which she concentrated on getting things organised. Not that Adam and the staff had done a bad job so far, but she liked to be in control. She took Melissa with her to town to purchase their personal stores for the journey. Several cart loads would be delivered to the Pride and Unicorn which were at the Stockley Shipping Company dock in the Thames Basin.

They did not need to take furniture. A missive from Canning informed them that a house had been procured and furnished. Even so, Caroline insisted that their own bed be loaded onto the Pride of Purbeck along with dinner services and Roland's cooking equipment.

Enough weapons were loaded onto both ships to supply a small army along with Marty's weapons' chest. Marty, having read the brief, realised that the residence would have to be an armed compound. He planned to have a company of marines in attendance as well as the Shadows. To make his marines more effective he had all their Baker rifles converted to percussion cap actions, issued Francotte revolvers to the officers and warrants and percussion cap, cavalry pistols to the marines. This increased their fire power and alleviated the need to carry flints and priming powder. Each man could carry a bag of cartridges and caps comfortably.

The Shadows all had revolvers and Sam stepped up to replace Billy as a full-time member. Hector inherited the fighting collar from Troy. At three years old he was fully grown and weighed in at a fit seventy-five pounds of solid muscle. He was fiercely protective of his pack and followed Marty everywhere.

The other passengers aboard the Unicorn were Sebastian Ashley-Cooper, Sir Raymond Johnson – Chargé d'Affaires, Peter De'ath – Secretary. It would be a small mission so they could move fast if they needed to. Sir Raymond was a former Guards captain and Peter De'ath a former lieutenant in the Logistics Corps.

Fully loaded and ready for sea, Marty and Caroline were met by Turner and Canning on the dockside.

"I wish you a good journey," Canning said, "and remember they are a murderous bunch."

"So are we," Caroline grinned, back to her old self now they were finally on their way.

"Nevertheless, be careful, they are not averse to using poison to remove unwanted people."

"George, we will be on our guard," Marty said.

Turner stepped up and kissed Caroline on the cheeks, "I will keep you updated on Beth's progress and when she is likely to get home. She will be due an extended leave after the mission is over."

"Long enough to visit us?" Caroline said.

"It's an eight-month round trip," Marty reminded her.

"At least," Wolfgang said as he joined them. "We need to catch the tide."

The Unicorn and Pride of Purbeck slipped out of harbour and started the first leg of their journey which would take them across the Atlantic to the northern tip of Brazil then back across with the trade wind to South Africa and Cape Town. Marty, Caroline, Melissa, Tabatha and Hannah were on the Unicorn along with the Shadows. The rest of their staff were comfortably accommodated on the Pride which also carried most of their baggage.

Marty and Caroline stood and watched the ships anchored in the Downs, then the white cliffs of Dover slip past. Then they were through the Dover Strait and easing more westward as they passed Hastings. As it was a nice day and very little sea was running, they had lunch on the quarterdeck.

"It seems strange not having Garai with us," Caroline said as they looked across the deck to Antton, Matai, Sam and Chin sat together eating their lunch. Garai was with Beth in South America. Roland was on the Pride as they wanted to avoid conflict with Wolfgang's chef Federico who was as temperamental as Roland was calm. Sam, who was also Marty's cox, could eat with the crew if he wanted but chose to stay with his brother Shadows. Adam was, naturally, serving them.

Wolfgang had the watch and paced the weather side of the deck, it being his domain. He looked up at the admiral's pennant flying above. *About time too,* he thought as he automatically checked the set of the sails and the way she was being steered. He had no wife. Which was not to say he was in any way celibate, rather he had a string of ladies he socialised with when in port.

He scanned the deck and wondered when Marty would start weapons practice. The modified rifles had arrived only a couple of days before they sailed. Delivered by a harassed gunsmith who had been given the commission. The new revolving chamber pistols were untried by the officers and warrants as well. They had plenty of time as it would take at least six weeks to sail to Cape Town and another four weeks to get to Burma. That was assuming they could keep up an average of ten knots and the weather was favourable all the way, which he very much doubted.

"Mr Longstaff, mind your braces!" Wolfgang shouted.

He smiled as Lieutenant Longstaff jumped to order the men to tension the braces. It paid to keep them on their toes.

He frowned, he was a fourth lieutenant and a midshipman short, as young Brazier and Donaldson were running the Fox for Beth. He considered his options. He could bring young Sterling up to acting fourth, but he was really not ready. Apart from that he was out of options for raising anyone from the crew to midshipman.

They would be passing Gibraltar and he wondered if they visited the peninsula, could they persuade Commander in Chief of the Mediterranean fleet to part with a couple of likely candidates.

"It's not a bad idea, there are always young lieutenants looking for a berth on a frigate and it would only delay us a couple of days," Marty said when Wolfgang broached the subject. "Only thing is, Sir Graham Moore may take the opportunity to offload a pair of wasters.

"Do you know him?"

"I do. He has a good record as a fighting sailor and was First Lord of the Admiralty between '16 and '20."

They decided it was worth a try and sailed into Gibraltar to find the flagship in port.

"Admiral Stockley. What brings you to these parts? Has Turner more skulduggery for you in Greece?" Moore greeted Marty and Wolfgang when they visited him.

"Not this time. I'm on my way to Burma as Ambassador."

"Good grief, Canning must be worried if he is sending you." He walked across his cabin and indicated they should join him around the dining table. "Lunch is about to be served, I am sure there is enough for three."

As soon as they sat, stewards set a cold table. Beef, pork, chicken, a pie, cheeses, slices of ham, pickles, chutneys and fresh shore bread. Glasses of Spanish Rioja were served.

"Get stuck in, I don't stand on ceremony," Moore commanded.

They helped themselves and munched away happily as they chatted. Moore told Marty the latest happenings in the Mediterranean and how the Greeks were fighting amongst themselves over how and by who, they should be ruled.

Marty in turn told him of the mission and then said, "Which brings me to the reason we stopped by. Because of an operation in South America, we are a fourth and a mid. short. We were wondering if you had anybody that you want to put forward?"

"As it happens my tenure here is about to end and there are a couple of young men who I would like to advance." He smiled at Wolfgang. "Captain Ackermann, you have a reputation for training excellent officers and there are few opportunities these days where they can hone their skills in active ships."

Wolfgang bowed his head at the compliment.

"As it happens, I do have a young man who has just passed his lieutenant's board and a request from an associate ashore to take his youngest son as a midshipman. I was going to put them on ships in the Mediterranean, but I think they would benefit more from sailing with you."

He rang a bell, and a steward came in. "Ask Midshipman Eden to attend us." He turned to Wolfgang, "Eden is the prospective lieutenant. He has an excellent record as a mid. and passed for lieutenant two months ago."

There was a knock at the door and the sentry announced, "Midshipman Eden, Sah!"

"Enter."

"You wanted to see me, Sir?" The young man who walked in through the door was probably nineteen or twenty years old. Of slightly more than medium height, broad shouldered and slim waisted with dark brown hair tied back navy style. Marty noticed he had ice blue eyes and a stare that made you feel he was looking through you.

"Jonathan, this is Admiral Stockley and Captain Ackermann of the Unicorn. They are on route to Burma and have a vacancy for a fourth lieutenant."

Marty and Wolfgang noted the use of the lad's first name. The young man looked concerned.

"Is there a problem?" Marty asked.

"Sorry, Sir. But I was under the impression the Unicorn was no longer a navy ship."

"Aah, that," Marty said. "Sit down and I will explain."

Ten minutes later.

"Oh, I see, so I would be listed as sailing on HMS Silent and accrue sea time."

"Exactly," Wolfgang said.

"Do you expect to see any combat in Burma?"

"Almost certainly," Marty said, then added, "The Burmese pirates are an ongoing problem in the area."

"When will I start?"

"Today, do you have a uniform?"

"Yes, Sir. I bought a full set in London when I passed my board."

"Then get into uniform and be ready for when we leave for our ship in half an hour."

When Eden had left Marty asked Moor, "You have interest in the lieutenant?"

Broad smiled. "He is my nephew, my wife's brother's youngest son."

"We will look after him," Wolfgang said.

"Hone him. He has potential but is too willing to lean on my patronage. Make a good officer of him and I will be in your debt." He coughed then added, "I will send a message to my associate to have the boy delivered to you in the morning before the tide. His name is Peter Woakes, and his father is the owner of the biggest ship building company on the peninsula."

The next morning a boat pulled up beside the Unicorn. It was immaculately turned out and looked brand new. In it was fourteen-year-old Peter Woakes. He looked belligerent and obviously didn't want to be there. His baggage was sent up and he was ushered up the steps by his father.

"Get up there and be a man," his father chided and cuffed him around the back of the head. The boy climbed the steps and stood at the top looking around the deck worriedly. His father followed him up.

Wolfgang met him and spoke with him briefly, took a purse and a letter from him after which the man departed, Marty watched on from the quarterdeck. Wolfgang rejoined him and passed him the letter.

"He has indentured him to the navy? What did he do?"

"He got in with a bad crowd and stole money from his father to buy drink. The last straw was when he was found abed with the daughter of the Madam of the Seven Veils."

The Seven Veils was a notorious brothel.

"The girl was following in the family tradition?"

"Maybe, she was fifteen and her mother demanded he marry her or pay a large amount in compensation. The father blames his wife, apparently, she has spoiled him since he was a baby."

"Did she, and does she know what his father has done?"

Just then furious shouting came from below.

"If I may, Sir," Fourth lieutenant Eden said with a salute, "The mids. are my responsibility."

Marty nodded. The lad had made a good start.

Eden went below to the cockpit where he found an exasperated Quinton Stirling confronting a tantrum-throwing Woakes. The boy was lying on a cot, thrashing his arms and legs and had gone red in the face.

"He refuses to do anything, Sir, and when I told him it was an order, he started on like this."

"Get a bucket of water," Eden said.

A bucket was fetched and handed to the lieutenant who calmly and without emotion poured it over the screaming boy's head.

The screaming stopped and was replaced by coughing.

"Stand up."

"No,"

"Stand up or I will order a mate to carry you to the main deck where you will be bent over a gun and caned."

"I don't want to be here."

"Hard luck, your father has signed you over to the navy and you can make life hell for yourself or cooperate and have a good time."

"He has no right to—"

"He has every right; you are fourteen years old. You have no rights until you are twenty-one. Now stand up."

Woakes stood, slouched.

"Stand up straight." The order was emphasised by a firm grip on an ear. "Better. Mr Stirling is the senior mid and as such he is your immediate superior and you will do as he orders. I am Fourth Lieutenant, and it is my job to teach you discipline and the manners becoming a gentleman in waiting. You will obey all orders from your superiors without question or delay. I will teach you the required mathematical and literary skills required of an officer. You will be assigned a sea daddy who will teach you the technicalities of sailing. That is, how to knot, splice, reef and steer. Now most mids have had at least two years' sea time by your age so you have a lot of catching up to do."

Woakes had tears running down his face.

The fourth lieutenant turned to Quinten. "How old were you when you joined, Quinten?"

"I was ten, Sir."

"Did you cry a lot?"

"Only because I was homesick, Sir."

"Then you can provide comfort to Peter and tell him about the adventures that you have had."

Lady Caroline took advantage of the brief stop. She and Melissa, escorted by Matai and Chin, went on a shopping tour. They didn't buy much, a pistol for Melissa being the biggest item.

"Is there any chance the Leonidas will stop here?" Melissa's eyes told how much she missed James.

"No, my dear, they are based in Crete so will not get to this end of the Mediterranean until their mission is over."

Tears welled and Melissa struggled to control herself. Caroline gave her the time she needed then said, "This is the lot of a sailor's wife. We have to bear the separations which make the time together that much sweeter."

"I know but it is hard knowing I probably will not see him for three years."

"I will make you a wager," Caroline looked out towards the Unicorn, "we will be on our way home before then. From what I know of the rulers of Burma we will not be welcome, and they will try to rid themselves of us one way or another. Keep your gun close and make sure it is loaded and capped at all times."

"What will Martin do?"

"What he does best. Cause as much trouble for our foes and competitors as possible."

The Winner

The ships sailed and Wolfgang watched his new fourth. He wanted to know how well he worked with the men and the mids. Come midday he had him run a sextant class to set their position. The new mid had no clue what to do with a sextant and Eden was patient with him. He had Stirling demonstrate how to find the angle between the sun and the horizon. Then helped Woakes try it for himself. The boy was bright if moody and spoilt and picked up the principles quickly. Then it was noon, and they took the readings for real.

The old mids, Stirling and Hepworth calculated their position and were within a mile or two of the master. Woakes had yet to learn the intricacies of the mathematics and looked on, interested. He asked questions which Stirling or Eden answered.

So far so good, Wolfgang smiled to himself.

That afternoon he had the men practising sail evolutions. His passengers sat under a canopy rigged on the quarterdeck watching them with interest. Lady Caroline waited until they had finished then asked, "May we fence for a while, Captain?"

"Please, feel free. I will have a space cleared aft of the mainmast."

He was not surprised to see Melissa take up a small sword and take her guard. What did surprise him was that Matai and his wife were practising knife fighting. The Caribbean woman was good, and Matai had his work cut out to beat her. When he did, Tabetha laughed and kissed him.

Sam's wife stepped up next and she had two nasty-looking curved knives which he recognised as being from

Indonesia. Curved like the fangs of a wolf, the sharp edge was on the inside of the curve and she held them with the blades down her forearms; the sharp edges forward. Matai grinned, took a second knife from his belt and held them the same way.

This was a new technique for Wolfgang who was used to holding a blade forehanded. That is, with the blade protruding from his fist so that his thumb could lay along the back edge. He had always thought that only amateurs held the blade downwards. He could see the advantage with the curved blade. Blocking was easier with the backhand grip and a backhand slash looked to be quite effective.

Marty joined him.

"Melissa has improved tremendously. She nearly had Caroline there."

"I was watching Sam and Hannah."

"Oh? What are they up to." Marty watched the pair for a long moment. "She must have gotten those knives from Garai. He likes them as they force a different style of fighting."

"She did and he taught her how to use them," Sam said from where he stood behind Marty's left shoulder. He had Hector on a line to stop him from joining in.

"Those blades aren't designed for stabbing, but they can cause terrible damage if you slash with them."

"She has dem tiger's claws from India as well," Sam said.

Marty was about to make a facetious comment about Hannah being a scratcher when Mary appeared. She talked to a deckhand, and he climbed up the main mast and out along the mainsail yard where suspended a biscuit tin lid from two lengths of string, so it hung clear of the sail.

"This should be interesting," Wolfgang said.

Mary paced off fifteen dainty steps and turned with a pistol in her right hand. Marty could see it was a Durs Egg under and over tube lock pistol. It was a novel design that had originally been a flintlock but since converted using a system patented by Joseph Manton. The pistol had two locks, one for each barrel, set either side of the frame. Instead of priming pans, the gun had priming holes that carried a brass tube of fulminate of mercury that reached into the chamber. Care had to be taken that you did not accidentally fire the gun by crushing the tube.

Mary raised the gun, cocking the right-hand hammer with her thumb as she did so. She steadied herself and squeezed the trigger. The tin lid swung as the .44-inch calibre ball smacked through it about an inch in from the top right-hand corner. She frowned, then raised the gun again, cocking the left-hand hammer. Her second shot hit the lid just right of centre.

"Good shot!" Marty called.

Mary smiled and waved to him then reloaded. Her next two shots were close to the second.

Melissa finished fencing with Caroline and the pair joined Mary. They were both very interested in the gun as Mary only got it a few days before they sailed. Melissa had her new gun and they compared them. They were similar, both had under and over barrels, of around the same length. Melissa's was heavier at .6-inch calibre and was percussion cap fired rather than tube fired like Mary's.

"How about a little competition?" Marty called.

"The men want to bet on us," Caroline whispered to the others, then called back, "Certainly, who will be the judge?"

"Antton!"

Antton was minding his own business splicing a loop on the end of a cable and looked up to see what his boss wanted.

"Judge the ladies' shooting contest," Marty called.

Antton put aside his work and walked over to the ladies. "We need a better target than that old tin. Give me a moment to set one up."

He found a length of 2x4 inch wood and lashed it to the rail, then took a lump of chalk and drew a 2-inch dot on it at around head height before knocking in a tack in the centre. He then paced off ten steps and drew a line on the deck.

"Who wants to go first?"

Caroline stepped forward. She had her Manton sixty-calibre muff pistols. She toed the line and took her stance side on as if she were duelling. She held the gun down, it was already cocked, her finger lay alongside the trigger guard.

Marty bet Wolfgang that Caroline would win as she was most used to her weapon. Wolfgang bet on Mary as he had seen her shoot and Gordon McGivern, the first lieutenant, took a punt on Melissa. The crew placed bets amongst themselves.

Sebastian and the other embassy staff joined in the fun making and taking bets. In the end a significant amount of money was at stake

Caroline took a breath and raised her pistol, sighted through the iron V backsight, and focussed her eye on the brass foresight which she placed slightly below and to the left of the target centre. Compensating for the slight roll of the ship, she slipped her finger through the trigger guard and squeezed.

The big bullet slapped into the plank on the edge of the dot, high and right at two o'clock. Caroline frowned, that was practically a miss in her book.

Mary went next, the order having been chosen by lots. She knew how to shoot and practised regularly. As before, she cocked her piece as she raised it, steadied, and pulled the trigger as she had been taught. Her ball hit the edge of the target at nine o'clock. She had jerked the trigger and she turned away muttering, "Squeeze the bloody thing you fool!"

Melissa toed the line; she could feel the anticipation of the men that had bet on her like a cloak hanging from her shoulders. She did just what James had taught her. It was an unknown gun so she assumed that it would kick up and right and compensated accordingly. Her hand shook as she pulled the trigger. The ball struck the target at twelve o'clock on the edge of the circle.

"It is a three-way tie!" Antton judged. "They shoot again."

This time Melissa got to shoot first. She chose to reload the right-hand barrel of her gun as that was the one with the sight mounted on it. *Focus, girl!* she told herself as she toed the line. She cocked the weapon. Then slowly raised it to eye level, focussed on the fore sight, compensating for recoil and squeezed the trigger gently.

BANG. The gun fired and the cloud of smoke from the barrel temporarily obscured the target. It blew away and she could see she had hit it at three o'clock about an inch from the middle. A cheer went up from her supporters.

Mary went next. She too reloaded so she could use the same barrel. She brought the gun to the ready, aimed and fired. The bullet flew true and hit the target slightly above and a quarter inch closer than Melissa's. Another cheer went up along with some groans.

Caroline stepped up having reloaded her single barrel. She toed the line, cocked her piece, and brought the gun up to the ready. You could see her take a breath, hold it and then gently squeeze the trigger. The bullet hit and Antton stepped forward. He used a piece of string to measure the distance from the tack at the centre of the target to the centre of each bullet to cancel out the differences in calibre.

"Lady Caroline and Mary are drawn, they shoot again." he cried.

Marty laughed; this was just the entertainment the ship needed.

"If I did not know it was impossible, I would think your good wife did that on purpose," Wolfgang grinned.

Sebastian stepped up to join them.

"My money is on Caroline."

"You are biased," Wolfgang said.

"I've seen her shoot."

"Caroline is going first. Antton flipped a coin and she won."

Caroline had indeed called heads and the George IV penny had landed in her favour. She stepped up to the line. The crew held its breath.

She took her time before she raised the gun to the ready, waiting until the ship's rhythm suited her. She fired. It was close to the centre at one o'clock.

Mary took her place, toeing the line. She licked her thumb and used it to wet the foresight, then brought the gun up. She too took her time and held her breath when she aimed. She pulled the trigger.

CLICK.

The gun misfired. She had to change the cap. The tension mounted as she took her stance again.

BANG.

Antton stepped forward.

It was very close and Antton took out his string again. He measured to the centre of Mary's bullet and asked a random crewman to verify his accuracy. He then swung the string around to the hole Caroline's bullet had made. He swung the string through it two or three times and had the crewman check it.

"Mary wins by an eighth of an inch."

Cheers and groans in equal parts echoed around the ship.

Caroline hugged Mary and congratulated her. Marty joined them.

"That was fine shooting by all three of you. Well done, Mary. You cost me a guinea."

"Who bet on me?"

"I did," Wolfgang said from behind her.

Caroline did a double take. Was there something between them? Was the look Wolfgang was giving her softer than she would expect? She looked at Mary who was looking boldly back at him.

Marty was oblivious and stepped in to hold Mary's arm high confirming Antton's announcement.

"The winner!"

Storm

The cruise down to the Canaries was uneventful. Both ships enjoyed the fair winds and moderate seas. They made excellent time and averaged almost three hundred land miles a day and after only six days at sea didn't need to replenish their fresh stores. They turned southwest to follow the trade wind to northern Brazil. A leg of just over two and a half thousand miles.

It all started well, the weather was fair and the wind favourable as one would expect from the trades. But then the lookout cried, "Deck there. There's a mass of clouds coming up on the port quarter."

Wolfgang climbed the ratlines with Arnold Grey, the master, to check it.

"That has come off Africa. It's the hurricane season in the Caribbean and that might be the seed of one," Arnold said.

"Is it a hurricane now?" Wolfgang said.

"No, it won't turn into one, if it does, until it gets to the Caribbean. It's just what them meteorologist fellers call a storm front, but it looks pretty strong, so we have to be careful."

It was indeed strong and developing into a full-blown storm. The area of low pressure had formed over The Gambia and had moved west out to sea. The South Equatorial Current, which was helping them make the crossing, was warm and helped fuel it with energy. It was uncommon for a storm to be that far south but not unknown.

"If we steer south to avoid it, we risk running into the doldrums," Wolfgang told Marty as they discussed what to do.

"We can't risk that, the window to get anything done in Burma is closing all the time and we need to get there as fast as possible. Get the Pride up to hailing distance."

By the time the Pride was close enough to hail the barometer had dropped an inch.

"We will ride the storm out," Marty bellowed using a speaking trumpet. "Try to stay close. If we get separated, we will rendezvous in Cape Town."

They could see the dark clouds catching them up slowly, lightning flickered along its front edge and thunder rumbled. The crew prepared. Safety lines were strung along the deck, and preventer stays fitted to the masts. Safety chains were fitted to the spars and storm sails prepared for hoisting.

"The wind along the front edge will be from the north but the waves will be running more to the southwest. We should be able to keep the sea on our stern until we get right into it," Arnold said.

Wolfgang knew all that but let Arnold confirm it anyway. He looked up and saw the pennant was swinging a little more to port. The anti-cyclone would disrupt the trade wind as it passed over them as it rotated withershins. If they passed right through the centre, they would see winds from the north followed after a brief still period by wind from the south. Anywhere either side and it would be more interesting.

The waves and wind picked up in equal measure. Wolfgang ordered a reef in the mains and topsails. A half hour later he ordered the mains taken in and another reef in the topsails. Twenty minutes after that he ordered the topsails double reefed, and the gallants taken in. The sea was now, what Arnold called, 'large'."

Marty stayed below with Caroline. It was not his usual habit in a storm at sea, but he felt that he should give her and the household his support.

"Will it get worse?" Caroline asked.

"Probably," Marty said, as the ship started to spiral.

"Ugh, that is horrible," Mary, who had come into their cabin, gasped.

"Caused by the waves travelling in a slightly different direction to us," Marty explained. "It should get better."

Mary lurched across the room to the washbasin and noisily threw up. The smell didn't help and triggered Melissa who had been quietly sitting in the corner.

"Oh lord," Caroline said and went to help the stricken women. Marty called for Adam who arrived with a bucket and mop. "This is fun," he quipped as he mopped up the mess and presented Melissa with her own bowl.

"We've had it easy until now," he teased.

Melissa said a very rude word that one would not expect a lady to know.

Marty put on his tarpaulin coat and hat and went up on deck. It was blowing a fierce and unforgiving gale, the waves mountainous. As he had predicted they were forced to run before it as the swell and the wind were coming from almost the same direction. That turned the corkscrew motion, that made so many sick, into a more manageable up and down with some wallowing to make it interesting.

"What is Arnold predicting?" he yelled at Wolfgang.

"That we should hit the eye sometime today. The barometer dropped another inch."

"Anyone hurt?"

"Not yet."

"I can take a watch if you want to go below and get some rest."

If anyone else had offered, they would have been refused outright, but as it was Marty, who he trusted with his life and ship, he agreed.

"Call me if anything breaks."

Marty grinned and shooed him away. He automatically looked up to the pennant and tell-tales on the storm sails. Little more than scraps of canvas, they kept the ship moving so they could keep her from broaching.

Most of the hands were below. Not that they were dry, the constant working of the timbers opened up seams and let the water drip down onto the gundeck. A sensible man put his waterproof coat over himself if he wanted to sleep dry-ish.

He looked for the Pride. It was as dark as a witch's soul and he couldn't see her at all. He searched the area she should be in with a night glass but still no luck. He sighed, she was a good ship and well handled by an expert crew. *She will be fine,* he told himself.

He had been on watch for at least two hours when the wind started to drop. They had reached the eye of the storm, and this is when the unwary got hurt. Marty wasn't one of those. The wind might be down to a more manageable level but as soon as the eye passed over them it would come back as fierce as before but in the opposite direction.

He looked up. There was a well of stars above him and he could see that the eye was quite large. The swirling mass of cloud that surrounded it was visible and several miles' wide. He had time to manoeuvre.

"Hands above to wear ship!" A thunder of feet was his answer as the men responded to the call.

"Bring her around to head into the waves," he said when he judged it safe to do so and the pennant indicated that the wind was swinging through east to south.

"Aye, aye, Admiral," the main helmsman said.

"Wear ship!"

The four men manning the big double wheel worked in unison and it spun around.

The top men and deck crew responded as he expected. professionally and with alacrity. The ship swung around, wallowing as the waves hit the beam. Then they were around and the sails pulling.

A flash of lightning.

"Hard to starboard!" Marty yelled and leaped to help with the wheel because in that flash he had seen the Pride half a cable, dead ahead, and beam on to them.

The ship groaned as she turned, canting over at the demand from the big rudder. A storm sail blew out with a bang from the strain. He watched, wide eyed, as the Unicorn's bowsprit passed over the Pride's quarterdeck and stern rail. The ship shuddered slightly as they caught her a glancing blow on the port quarter.

He rushed to the rail and could clearly see her skipper in the next flash of lightning, and waved. He sent a man to check for damage.

Wolfgang appeared.

"It was the Pride. I spotted her just in time."

"You tossed me out of my cot."

Marty laughed and then remembered to resume course.

"Steer north. Get that storm sail replaced." He turned back to Wolfgang and realised he was in pyjamas under his tarpaulin coat.

"The wind is almost coming from due south now. It's about to get rough again."

The crew man returned and reported that there was no damage apart from some scraped paint.

"I will take the watch!" Wolfgang shouted as the wind increased.

"Get dressed first or you will catch a cold!" Marty laughed.

The morning saw them on the back edge of the storm, the worst of it over. The sky slowly brightened as the bank of clouds moved away to the west. The waves that had been so big overnight started to shrink and get further apart.

The sun was beginning to break through when the lookout called.

"Deck there, I can see the Pride three points off the starboard quarter. She is signalling."

"Mr Hepworth, go aloft and see if you can make out what she is saying," Wolfgang ordered.

Hepworth grabbed a telescope and ran up the ratlines, over the futtock shrouds and settled on the gallant spar. He scanned the horizon and then centred his lens on the Pride.

There was something not quite right about her. A gust of wind brought the signal into view.

"She is signalling that she needs assistance! She looks a bit odd."

She did indeed look a bit odd as they closed with her. She was down by the stern and wallowing, her pumps working continuously.

"Oh bugger, we must have holed her," Marty said.

Wolfgang stood beside him. "Get the carpenter and his mates ready to go across and we will put her in our lee."

"Aye, aye, Captain," Gordon McGivern said.

"I assume you want to go over with them?"

Marty didn't answer, he was already heading to the entry port.

On board the Pride everything had an air of calm, but Marty sensed the stress. He went below with the carpenter and Captain Dunbar.

"Your ship has two or even three layers of oak, ours is only a merchantman with one thin layer, when you glanced off us you sprung three planks in our stern."

Marty could see the damage. Two of the planks were under the waterline and water was pouring in despite the feathered canvas that had been put on the outside. One of them was clearly broken and would have to be replaced.

"Get everything and everybody you can to the starboard side. Shift the cargo if you have to and move the guns."

Men rushed to do his bidding and he called for more hands from the Unicorn. Slowly the ship acquired a list to starboard and the planks were lifted above the waterline – just. The pumps made headway and the gap widened as the stern rose.

A platform was created for the carpenters to work on and slung over the side. The Unicorn held station to keep them in her lee and to protect her from the swell. The carpenter and his mates went down onto the platform and started to remove the broken plank. Now was a critical time, as any increase in the size of the waves, they would run the risk of losing the Pride altogether. A new plank was brought over from the store of spare timbers on the Unicorn and shaped. The carpenters skilfully wielding razor-sharp adzes. Once it was ready, it was lowered over the side and fitted into place with long iron nails. The sound of hammering and sawing continued until dark when lamps were lit and the process of making the Pride watertight continued.

By midnight the planks had been reset or replaced and the seams caulked. A tired but happy crew of carpenters were served a double ration of rum and the Pride started the process of getting back on an even keel.

They stayed close together making four or five knots until Marty could see that the Pride was swimming normally and they had stopped pumping.

"Are you ready to make full sail?" Marty called across.

"Aye, we are. But I would appreciate a moderate rate of increase, just to be sure."

Marty agreed and asked Wolfgang to gradually increase sail to their full cruising speed.

Caroline and the household came on deck to watch and to enjoy the morning sunshine.

"Is our ship sound again?" she asked.

"She should be unless there was some damage we couldn't see."

The topmen loosed the mainsails and they filled with a boom. The Unicorn accelerated gently and the Pride kept up, a cable astern and off their port quarter. Wolfgang looked back at them – waiting until Dunbar came forward and gave a thumbs-up.

"Set topsails and gallants," McGivern ordered when he got the nod from Wolfgang.

Soon they were making a steady twelve knots. The wind was on their port quarter and the waves, rolling and well spaced.

Caroline walked to the rail and stood by Keith Farrell, the third lieutenant.

"Tell me about when Bethany was on the Unicorn."

"Oh, Milady, she was fierce," he said. "She stood on the deck when we sprung her trap on the four schooners rifle in hand picking off their officers like it were a duck shoot."

She could see his colour heighten as he spoke, and he was obviously proud of what her daughter had done.

"She organised the trap?"

"Aye, along with Garai and an agent on shore. She's a right chip of the old block."

Caroline had a thought.

"What was she wearing during the fighting?"

"Leather trousers and bodice." Farrell went even redder.

She chuckled. She knew why he blushed now.

"A chip off her great grandmother's block."

"Milady?"

"My great times five grandmother was a privateer. The Scarlet Fox. Heard of her?"

"Why yes, she was an associate of Henry Morgan and the scourge of the inquisition. She was your ancestor?"

"Yes, and I think my daughter has inherited her piratical tendencies."

Keith didn't answer as he was absorbed in the memory of Beth in those tight buckskin trousers. Caroline left him gazing out to sea. She would question Beth about the outfit next time she saw her.

São Luis

Despite the attentions of the carpenter and his mates the Pride was still leaking through a gap in her planking that had opened up since the repairs. They were having to pump her every two hours.

"We are going to have to get her into somewhere we can offload the cargo and dump her water, that leak is well below the waterline," Stan Hamble, the carpenter, reported to Marty and Wolfgang, after a shouted conversation with the Pride's carpenter.

The three went to the chart table and were joined by Arnold Grey.

"Is there is anywhere on the Brazilian coast that will serve?" Wolfgang asked Arnold after they explained what they were looking for.

"Saint Louis or São Luis is the closest and would serve. It's got beaches where we can haul her out. Salvador would be better but a lot further."

Wolfgang looked at Marty who nodded.

"Chart a course for São Luis." He turned to the carpenter. "Is speed a factor in how fast she leaks?"

"No, Sir. It's a stern plank almost down by the keel. So, keeping up a decent speed actually helps."

Marty cursed inwardly; this would take at least a week. *But then it's your own fault, if you had spotted her sooner—* Then he scolded himself, *I couldn't have spotted her sooner and may never have if it weren't for that bolt of lightning.*

He knew self-recrimination wasn't going to help. Accidents happen at sea, and they were lucky this one didn't cost them the Pride. They would just have to make up as much time as they could.

São Luis came up on the horizon just a point south of their heading. The town was named after the island it sat on, but as Marty noted from the chart it was more of a peninsula separated from the land by little more than a river. There were two inlets. The northern one was called Baia de São Marcos and the southern, Baia de São Jose. Arnold thought the northern one preferable as the town had a dock.

As Marty had a little Portuguese from during the war, he got the job of explaining to the local officials what they wanted to do.

"Temos de descarregar esse navio e repará-lo," Marty said in his best Portuguese.

The man looked at him for a long moment.

" Precisamos descarregar esse navio e repará-lo."

Marty was confused and repeated himself to which the man replied in exactly the same fashion.

"He is telling you how to say it in Brazilian Portuguese," a bystander said in English.

"Is it different?" Marty sighed.

"It is, maybe I can help. What is it you need to do?"

Marty explained and the man, who he found out was called Max Cabral, a tobacco trader, explained to the official. The man replied curtly.

"The pig says that you can store your cargo in that warehouse over there and pull your ship on the beach to the east. I know it, it's used for careening. He wants to charge you a hundred reals. He is robbing you."

"I will pay him fifty,"

"He says not a real less than seventy-five."

"Sixty-five."

The deal was done. They didn't shake hands as the official just stalked off.

"Friendly chap," Marty laughed.

Max laughed along with him, and Marty offered to buy him a drink for his trouble. As they were sitting sipping glasses of Caipirinha, the Unicorn's longboat came alongside the dock and Caroline, Tabetha and Mary stepped ashore. Marty waved and they came over. The men stood and Marty made the introductions.

"Max, this is my wife, Caroline. Caroline, this is Max who speaks perfect English and Brazilian Portuguese."

Marty was surprised when he slurred a little. His tongue felt numb.

"Delighted to meet you, Max. What have you two been drinking?" Caroline laughed.

"Caipirinha. It's our national drink."

Caroline picked up Marty's glass and tasted it.

"Lime, sugar and some kind of raw spirit?"

"Yes, it's cane spirit."

"No wonder my tongue is numb." Marty giggled.

Caroline beckoned to the boat and Sam came ashore.

"When my husband has finished his drink, please help him get back to the ship."

"Yes, Milady," Sam said, looking at Marty quizzically. He had never seen him drunk before. Max was also slightly tipsy but being more used to the concoction was not as worse for wear.

"We are going to look around the town," Caroline said.

"You, my friend, are a very lucky man," Max said as he watched the ladies walk away.

Caroline walked confidently through the ramshackle town with Mary and Tabetha either side of her. The three of them were dressed simply by London standards but stood out compared to the locals.

They wandered through the colonial-style building-lined streets, going into shops, and buying a few things. Fletcher, the purser, was taking care of the provisioning of fresh meat and vegetables so they ignored the many fruit and vegetable stalls apart from buying some oranges. The street food vendors called out to them, and they examined their wares, trying free samples. Mary took a liking to Mandioca frito or fried cassava chips and bought some wrapped in a leaf to snack on. Caroline and Tabetha shared a couple of Pastel de queijo which were deep-fried cheese pastries.

The people were friendly and curious as they didn't see many European women, as the bigger port of Rio de Janeiro was the entry point for the Portuguese and other Europeans. The local women wore white blouses and embroidered skirts which had a hoop that held it out from their hips. The men wore baggy trousers with a white shirt. Some wore ponchos as well.

The town wasn't very big, and they soon found themselves in less salubrious surroundings. The houses shabbier, and the roads less well cared for. Men on horseback road past. Bearded and unkempt they wore high leather boots rather than the sandals the common man wore. Some drove cattle and carried whips of plaited leather which they cracked above the animal's heads. Others carried a rope with a loop in the end which the ladies had no idea what was for. A crowd of men at a run-down cantina spotted them and started shouting and gesturing. The ladies coolly ignored them and walked on. The calls got louder and presumably more coarse. Four men left the tavern and followed them.

"We may have wandered into a bad part of town," Mary said.

"Indeed," Caroline agreed.

Two of the men ran past them and blocked their way forward. Gap tooth smiles cracked their dirty faces. They carried knives through the sashes around their waists.

Caroline's hand came out of her pocket with her muff pistol in it. There was a loud double click as she cocked it followed by the clicks of two other guns being brought to full cock.

"Saia do nosso caminho," (Get out of our way) Caroline said.

The men didn't move.

Caroline sighed; she didn't want to have to shoot the ape but was fully prepared to if she had to. She focussed on the one she thought was the leader and pointed the gun right between his eyes.

"Você realmente quer morrer?" (You really want to die?)

The man looked slightly unsure of himself than stiffened as the cat calls from the cantina grew louder.

Suddenly the two men were felled by a much larger man that appeared from nowhere and crashed their heads together. They slid senseless to the floor.

"Ladies," Matai bowed.

"Matai, I had it under control," Caroline said as she lowered her gun and made it safe.

"Marty doesn't want the place littered with corpses, well not until the Pride is repaired," Antton said as he and Chin appeared from behind her. A glance told her that the other two men were unconscious on the dirt road.

"How long have you been with us? No, that's a silly question. You were onshore waiting for us I suppose."

Antton just grinned, then glanced back towards the tavern. "I think it would be best if we moved on. That crowd is getting ugly."

As they moved off, the crowd of ten or so individuals at the cantina started after them. Matai drew his revolver and fired two shots into the dirt at their feet and one above their heads. The men stopped in astonishment. As far as they were concerned pistols only fired once. To see one fire three times was tantamount to witchcraft.

"That got them thinking; if I'm prepared to waste three shots to warn them how many would we be able to send if they really pissed us off," Antton said as they walked casually back to the nicer part of town.

The Pride was unloaded of people, guns, cargo, furniture, stores, water, and ballast until she was totally empty over the next two days. The people were housed on the Unicorn or ashore in cantinas, the goods stored in a warehouse which Marty posted marine guards on. She floated like a cork and still the offending plank was just below the waterline. The men towed her using the ship's boats to the beach a mile away where another ship had been hauled out for careening.

They unshipped her rudder and towed her backwards up the beach at high tide. Tackles had been rigged, anchored to trees and anchors that had been set in the sand for just this purpose by the people who did the cleaning. When the tide went out she was sitting with her stern high and dry with a slight list to starboard. The carpenters went to work.

Marty, who had woken up with a hangover that morning, after his drinking session with Max, watched them work. Stan came over after they had removed the plank and investigated the damage.

"You will be happy to know that your little collision didn't cause the plank to spring. Well not directly anyway."

"Really? What caused it then?" Marty said.

"These." Stan held out four copper nails. The points were still sharp. "Whoever put them in didn't put a rove on or peen them over, so they just worked loose. The jar of the collision might have accelerated it."

Marty was aghast, "That could have happened at any time!"

"Aye, it be by God's grace it ain't happened before. I got my boys checking the rest of the hull to see if there's anymore."

"How long?"

"We can get her off at the next high tide."

That was far quicker than Marty expected, and he returned to the Unicorn in better spirits.

That night Marty was roused from bed by Sergeant Bright.

"There's trouble at the warehouse, Sir."

Marty was up, dressed, and fully armed in a trice and led a squad of marines and the Shadows ashore. He could hear shouting and see the flickering light of torches in the vicinity of the warehouse.

"Form them up, Sergeant," he growled as the warehouse came into sight.

There was a largish group of, mostly, men gathered in front of the warehouse facing off against the four marines and their corporal who were stopping them getting to the doors.

Someone had gotten in, presumably through a side door or window, and was in the opening above the doors used for winching, waving what looked like one of Caroline's dresses.

"Fix bayonets and advance in line," he ordered. He pulled one of his pistols and took aim at the man in the opening. The shot rang out and the man fell to the ground, blood pooling in the cobbles.

The shot brought the attention of the mob to Marty and the marines. The Shadows had dispersed to take the crowd from different directions to confuse them. One man, who seemed transfixed by the sight of the body, let out a howl and ran at Marty waving a machete.

He got about halfway when there was a shot from the dark. He was picked up and thrown backwards in an elongated summersault, the back of his head and brains spraying out behind him.

A woman screamed and the crowd looked on, eyes wide.

The marines advanced. Cold determination in their eyes.

The corporal got his men lined up and bayonets glinted in the torchlight as they too advanced.

Marty glanced up at the opening. Antton was knelt in it, rifle at the ready. Screams from inside the warehouse told him where the rest of the Shadows were.

The next morning, the town mayor and the obstreperous official arrived. Max appeared and joined Marty.

"I heard there was some trouble last night and people got killed," the mayor said.

"Yes, two. They were trying to rob the warehouse."

The mayor puffed out his chest and started to rant. Marty calmly waited until he finished then looked around to see the Pride pull up at the dock. He watched armed marines line the route to the warehouse and the men start to reload and ballast her.

"What did he say?" he asked Max.

"He is angry you didn't call for the local militia to help you and that you killed a father and son."

"Tell him there is no formal treaty between Britain and Brazil since it became independent from Portugal. He is lucky I don't burn his town to the ground. They have insulted my wife and tried to steal from me. I hold him responsible."

The mayor went into another tirade. Marty looked bored by the whole performance, took out a handkerchief and waved it at the Unicorn. Her gun ports opened and the guns ran out.

The mayor's eyes went round, the muzzles of the guns looked like gateways to hell. The official looked astonished, and his mouth hung open. The mayor took off his hat and hit him with it babbling away angrily at the same time.

Max was laughing so hard he could hardly speak.

"He is asking him why he didn't know that one of the ships was a warship and is accusing him of incompetence. It's really funny because the official is his brother, and he gave him the job."

The brothers headed back into town. The mayor still berating his sibling and swiping at him with his hat. When he kicked him on the backside Marty joined in the laughter.

Cape Town

The Pride, now fully watertight, looked a picture as she sailed abeam of the Unicorn, her copper showing as she heeled in the wind. The carpenter's mates had found forty-three nails that had no rove fitted. The correction was simply to add a rove and knock the end down which they did as they found them.

Marty was angry at the shipbuilder who had obviously employed someone who was either incompetent or criminal. However, there was nothing he could do about it as she had been a prize and he had no idea who the builder was.

The trip across the South Atlantic was one of high rolling waves and steady trade winds. On a whim Marty asked Arnold to route them past St Helena.

"Why do you want to pass that God forsaken rock?" Wolfgang asked.

"Napoleon died there in '21. I heard about it before we left. Shelby diagnosed him with some kind of stomach cancer while we were taking him there, which, along with the climate, probably killed him. I just want to pay my respects."

Wolfgang shrugged. He never understood the relationship between the two men who had been implacable enemies. It would add a day to their journey.

Marty stepped up the weapon training for the household and embassy staff. All of the Shadows got involved and the ladies learnt some interesting new self-defence techniques. Over on the Pride the rest of the staff were also practising shooting, self-defence and sword work. Matai had volunteered to sail on her to oversee their training and he was evidently working them hard.

On the Unicorn, Chin was teaching the ladies some unarmed combat. He focussed on simple effective moves to counter typical attacks on women. He showed them how to pin their hair up Chinese style with two long hairpins and how to use those hairpins as weapons. He also showed them how to perform a hip throw, a basic arm throw and a leg throw, how to clap their hands over their opponents' ears to disorientate them and attack the eyes, groin and solar plexus.

Marty joined in and found himself on his back on the deck to the great amusement of the crew. He also polished up his fighting skills. He was a natural knife fighter and an excellent swordsman. However, his close combat skills needed improvement. He had Chin teach him quánfã, which some called Chinese boxing, but it was more than that, Chin explained.

"Boxing only uses the fist. Quánfã uses the whole hand. If we bring in the feet, we are moving towards Kung Fu which is taught by the Shaolin monks. You do not have the flexibility for Kung Fu."

He demonstrated some kicks to the head which startled even Marty who had practised with him for years.

"You're right. I couldn't get my leg that high using a block and tackle," Marty laughed.

"I could," Melissa said from behind him.

Marty stepped aside and beckoned her forward.

"Could you teach her?"

"You practise dance with Lady Caroline?"

"Ballet."

"I taught Bethany so I can teach you."

That was news to Marty.

"When?"

"I started teaching her when she was eight years old. She is very adept now."

Marty shook his head. He wished he had paid more attention to what his children were doing as they grew up.

Chin soon had them shadow fighting, running through the basic moves then moving on to more advanced. Several crew and Caroline joined in and soon the main deck rang to the cries of people punching in unison.

It took seventeen days to get to St Helena and Marty had Wolfgang slow and fire a twenty-one-gun salute and dip their colours as they passed. The crew manned the yards in their best white shirts. From the shore it looked extraordinary. The governor first thought it was for him but then saw the colours dip to half-mast, they were flying the French flag under the union flag.

The Unicorn passed close enough he could pick out her name using a telescope.

"I will write to the admiralty."

His clerk had the navy list of ships and searched through it. "Did you say she was the Unicorn?"

"Yes, damn them."

"She is listed as being sold off. She isn't a navy ship."

"Well, who the hell is sailing around in a fully armed frigate?"

Their respects paid, they set course for Cape Town, another week's sailing away. The lookouts were wary of storms coming up behind them and random squalls. At their latitude they were not as frequent or as large as the storms south of Cape Horn, but they could still drive you south into the ice fields.

The wind was verging on a gale and whipped the tops of the waves into spume and spray. The sailing was exhilarating for the officers and crew, but some of the civilian passengers were not so thrilled. Mary was especially prone to seasickness and that caused Wolfgang to worry.

Marty and Caroline both noticed he was especially solicitous of her and even went with her down to the Orlop deck to consult with Mr Shelby. Shelby, the ship's physician, was accompanied by his wife Annabelle, also a medical doctor, and their new-born baby boy Thomas, who was born two weeks before they joined the Unicorn. Shelby attended the birth along with a midwife. It had been an easy one by all accounts and the happy family re-joined the ship to the cheers of the crew. Luckily Thomas was one of those babies that hardly ever cried. Probably because his mother had ample milk and cared for his needs without having to be prompted by squalling.

Wolfgang and Mary arrived in the surgery to find Shelby tending to a dislocated shoulder. The seaman had a strip of leather between his teeth and was firmly in the grasp of a pair of loblolly boys. Shelby placed a wooden ball under his arm and used it to lever the shoulder back into place. He looked up and saw them, taking in Mary's condition in a glance.

"Annabel is through there," he said kindly and gestured to a door.

They knocked and heard Annabelle call, "Come in!" She sounded cheerful and when they entered, they found her feeding Thomas.

Wolfgang looked embarrassed and she chided him, "This is the most natural thing in the world, I am not embarrassed by it, and neither should you be."

Wolfgang grinned sheepishly while Mary looked at Thomas adoringly. "Oh, what a handsome boy he is and growing like a weed!"

She sat next to Annabelle and the two talked babies. Wolfgang, seeing she had quite forgotten her seasickness, smiled and bowed his way out.

Shelby grinned at him over the head of the seaman he was fitting with a sling.

"Works nearly every time."

Wolfgang laughed then went to the injured man.

"Morris, isn't it?"

"Aye, Captain."

"How did it happen?"

"I lost me footing in the cross trees. Lucky I had a hold on the backstay, but me shoulder got a wrench as I dropped awkward like."

"But you didn't let go. That saved your life. Well done."

"He made it to the deck without help as well," Shelby added.

Morris looked happy at the praise.

Wolfgang looked to Shelby.

"How long does he need to be off duty?"

"Two weeks and then another two weeks on light duties."

"Ow, Cap'ain I don't need that long. It do feel better already."

"And it will pop out the first time you put pressure on it," Shelby interjected. "It needs to settle, so no climbing for two weeks!"

Marty was on the quarterdeck enjoying the feel of the ship as she raced eastward. Gordon McGivern had the watch, so Marty had the luxury of being a passenger. The steady climb up the backside of the large rolling waves followed by the moment the ship surged forward down the forward side was almost hypnotic. He smiled as spray from the bow hitting the rear face of the next wave blew back and spattered his face.

There was a scream.

"Man overboard! Starboard side!"

Marty spun and ran to the rail in time to see the head and shoulders of a man in the water rapidly disappearing aft. McGivern was yelling orders to bring the ship about. Without thinking, Marty ran aft, shedding his coat and shoes. He grabbed a cork fender as he passed the mizzen and launched himself over the stern.

The man was already half a cable behind them, and Marty could see him struggling to stay afloat as he passed over the top of a wave and out of sight. Marty swam as fast as he could, the fender bobbing along behind him, its rope looped around his waist.

Behind him the Unicorn struggled to turn into wind. Off to the side the Pride was reducing sail to slow to a stop under backed foresails. Both were trying to man boats.

He was getting tired by the time he reached the peak of the wave, but going down the back face was easier. He could hear the man shouting and he homed in on the sound. He saw him twenty feet away and put in a last spurt to reach him. Once he got close, he pulled the fender around in front of him and advanced on the man who was flailing his arms in an attempt to reach him. Marty shoved the fender into him and once the man had a hold of it, took a grip himself and relaxed.

"Admiral, thankee, thankee," the man spluttered.

"Filkins?" Marty asked as he recognised him.

"Aye, Sir."

"Relax, they will send a boat for us soon."

"I hope so, Sir. Before they get us."

"Who?"

Marty swivelled his head and saw a shiny grey fin approaching followed by two more.

"Are you cut?" he asked.

"I lost a couple of fingernails and they be bleeding a bit."

That explained the sudden appearance of the predators who could scent blood up to a quarter of a mile away. They were probably following the ship to feed on the garbage and when Filkins fell overboard, he left a trail that was as plain as day to them.

The lead shark came closer to investigate whether they were a meal or not. Marty ducked under the water as it approached and, in desperation, punched it square on the end of the nose. Shocked and a little disoriented, the shark swung away.

Marty came back to the surface. The sharks were circling about ten feet away.

"Watch them, if one moves in, try and punch or kick it on the nose. That seems to put them off."

A smaller one got brave and moved in and Filkins flapped his legs at it. The shark avoided him easily and re-joined its friends.

The water was cold, and they started to shiver now they were not expending energy staying afloat. The sharks circled a little closer. Marty was wondering where the hell the boats were.

"He did what?" Caroline cried when Wolfgang told her why they were stopping.

"Grabbed a fender and dove over the stern. He didn't hesitate."

"What are you doing?"

"The boat is manned and is on its way. The Pride has also manned a boat. One should reach them soon."

The boats were at sea but were having trouble finding the two men. The waves were high and unless they were all on the crests at the same time the small figures of two men in the water would be impossible to see.

Quinton Sterling was in charge of the boat and was the one who noticed the sharks heading purposefully away from the Unicorn. He hauled his rudder and followed them, shouting at the sole marine.

"Get that rifle ready."

It was standard practice for a marine to be aboard any boat for security and this one had joined as a matter of course.

Suddenly the bow man flung out an arm indicating they should steer slightly to port. He spotted them a moment later, fifty feet away. He kicked the marine and pointed at the sharks slowly closing in on the pair. The man stood and aimed.

If he makes this shot, he will be a bloody hero, Quinten thought as he urged the oarsmen to greater efforts.

"Put your backs into it, that's the admiral over there."

BANG, the marine fired.

Marty was concentrating on the sharks so did not see the approaching boat from the Unicorn or the one from the Pride coming in a bit further off. There was a bang and the closest shark thrashed as a hole appeared in its side under its dorsal fin. The other sharks reacted immediately, tearing into it in a feeding frenzy.

A rope landed across Marty's shoulder, and he tried to grab it with numb fingers. Realising he couldn't hold onto it he wrapped it around his forearm and clamped his arm against his body.

Moments later he was manhandled into the boat followed by Filkins. The two men were shivering and were wrapped in blankets. Then before they knew it, they were on the Unicorn's deck.

"Get them below now," Shelby said taking charge of the sodden men and as soon as they were in his domain. "Get those wet clothes off them and bring something hot for them to drink.

Once they were stripped Shelby and a loblolly boy rubbed them down briskly with towels, being rough to promote circulation. Then they were wrapped in towels.

Caroline appeared.

"Are they…?"

"They will be fine. They are very cold and need to warm up slowly."

Adam arrived with two large mugs of beef broth laced with sherry. The men cupped it in their hands and sipped it gratefully. Marty sensed rather than felt the Unicorn make way.

Gradually he stopped shivering and looked up at Caroline who had a look on her face that spoke of words that would be said later. Marty sighed. She led him back to their cabin once Shelby gave permission.

"What the hell were you thinking!" Caroline hissed as soon as the door closed.

"That he couldn't swim," Marty answered simply.

"You—"

He held her and she cried, partly in anger at her, impetuous over brave husband but more in relief. Marty said nothing. He just stroked her hair and held her until she had cried herself out.

"I'm tempted to tell you never to do that again, but I know it would do no good."

"I am what I am," Marty said and kissed her.

Their lovemaking was slow and loving and did more to return Marty's core temperature to normal than anything else.

Cape Town came up on the horizon and the two ships reduced sail to make the approach to the harbour as they rounded Robin Island. The city had grown since the last time they had been here and was showing signs of the wealth to be found in South Africa. The city was predominantly populated by the English and Boers, the Dutch-speaking Free Burghers. Any Africans were servants or slaves.

They anchored and presented their credentials to the officials. It was about half an hour before an invitation to visit the governor arrived.

"General, Sir Richard Bourke cordially invites Ambassador Viscount Stockley and his lady wife to dinner this evening." Caroline read from the letter she had opened even though it was addressed to Marty who was reading a copy of *Ivanhoe* by Walter Scott.

"I suppose we ought to, though I don't think the food will live up to Roland's standards," Marty said. "In any case we can catch up on the goings on here."

"What should I wear?"

"That emerald, green dress of yours is very pretty, why not wear that?"

"It does go well with my Indian jewels. We can take Melissa with us."

"She isn't family yet." Marty knew full well what the situation between his son and Melissa was and was trying to get a rise out of his wife.

"Oh tush. She is as good as. James and she are betrothed."

"Are they? He never asked me," Marty said, hiding a smile.

Caroline stopped searching through her trunk and gave him a long, flat, look.

"I'm sure he will as soon as we get back."

"I will give it some thought," Marty said and went back to his book. A garter hit him on the forehead.

"She can come if she is accompanied by Sebastian."

The ship's boat rowed them ashore and a carriage was waiting for them. Caroline and Melissa looked stunning as ever in complementary dresses. Marty wore his admiral's uniform with his honours on a sash and Sebastian wore his Rifles uniform complete with his Army Gold medal, Gold Cross with four clasps, Military General Service and Waterloo medals. They reached the residence and were ushered inside where they were met by Sir Richard, his wife Elizabeth, daughter Mary and her affianced, Dudley Montague Perceval.

"Greetings, Lord Martin. It has been a long time since we last met," Sir Richard said with a noticeable speech impediment caused by a wound to the jaw he received in the Anglo-Russian invasion of Holland in 1799.

"The Peninsula, I believe," Marty said, remembering the much younger quartermaster general he had met there.

The introductions taken care of, they moved to a drawing room that could have been straight out of an English country house. There Marty had the chance to talk to Dudley.

"I knew your father," Marty said.

"I know, you were there when he died." Spencer Perceval was assassinated in the hall of the house of commons.

"I am sorry I couldn't save him."

"He died doing what he loved best. Politics was his life."

"Yes, I hope we never experience another prime minister being assassinated. Do you have ambitions in that direction?"

"Oh, no, Sir. I am happy with my lot and the chance to marry Mary. Administration is what I want to do, especially under a man like Sir Richard who is a great reformer."

They sat down to dinner. Marty sat to Sir Richard's right and Caroline and Melissa bracketed Elizabeth. Sebastian and Dudley sat opposite each other.

"If I might make an observation. You are not a known diplomat, and your skills lie more on the side of intelligence gathering. How did you land the residency in Burma?"

"A good observation and an equally good question. The truth is the position is not without its perils. The Burmese king and his family are fond of using assassination to remove those who get in their way, and we expect their territorial ambitions westward to eventually lead to conflict with us. Add to the mix, France's consolidation of their Indo-Chinese holdings, China and Siam and we have a powder keg waiting to explode."

"Well, I wish you all the luck. That is one hornet's nest I wouldn't want to be in."

Marty laughed and produced a golden guinea out of seemingly thin air then made it disappear.

"The trick will be to make them think we are doing one thing when we will be doing something completely different." He reached out and appeared to take the guinea from Sebastian's ear, it disappeared again.

They were eating a soup course and Sir Richard suddenly exclaimed then laughed. There in his bowl was the golden guinea.

"Were you at Waterloo?" Duncan asked Sebastian looking at his medals.

"I was, as was Lord Martin who I fought beside."

"An admiral at Waterloo?"

"He was Wellington's head of intelligence. I was a lieutenant in the King's German Legion, and he was a captain then."

"So, you were on the line?"

"No, we fought at La Haye Saint. In the centre but ahead of the line."

Duncan would not let either go without their story of Waterloo.

The Longest Leg

They left Cape Town refreshed and resupplied. The SOF prided themselves on never having a man go down with scurvy so having plenty of fresh vegetables and citrus juice was important. So was fresh meat; a pair of bullocks were added to the manger.

This leg of the journey was some nine and a half thousand miles. They would follow the Antarctic circumpolar wind east before turning north past Mauritius to pick up the south equatorial wind that would take them, initially, west past the Seychelles. The wind circulated clockwise and would take them north parallel with the Sudanese coast then swing west past the southern tip of India. They would pass through the Ceylon Strait up the east coast of India to the Bay of Bengal and into the Andaman Sea. It was the long way round, but they would have the wind on their stern the whole way. They were aiming to dock at Yangon where they would transfer to river boats to take them up the Irrawaddy River to Ava. Another four hundred and eighty miles.

Marty estimated that it would take at least forty days to reach Ava and the residence. Far too long in his opinion but there was nothing he could do about it. So, they headed out of Cape Town and picked up the Antarctic wind.

The bonus for the passengers was that they got to see whales. The lookouts would call, and the passengers would crowd the rail.

"They are enormous!" Melissa gasped as she caught sight of the huge grey shapes two hundred yards of the beam.

"Humpbacks," Marty said and passed her a small telescope.

Huge spouts of water droplets shot up from their breathing holes.

"Look, they are keeping up with us," she cried.

"They can go faster if they have a mind to."

"Are they dangerous?"

"They can be if you threaten them, but we will keep our distance."

They watched the elegant beasts for an hour spotting at least one juvenile. Then they just disappeared.

"Where did they go?"

"My thought is that they dove down to the depths to feed," Marty said then added, "if we were further south near the ice fields, we would see seals."

A huge grey shape was seen cruising under the ship.

"Is that a whale?" Caroline asked.

"No, Ma'am, that be a shark. The one they call the Great White. That one be about fifteen foot long," a crewman said.

She shuddered as its cold dark eye seemed to turn on her from just below the surface.

It got warmer when they turned north until they swung west with the wind past the Seychelles, and it was more tropical. The weather did not threaten them at all. But as they rounded north again the lookout called.

"Deck there. Sails to the south."

"Could be an Indiaman," McGivern said.

Wolfgang frowned, his trouble sense was pinging.

"Mr Stirling, be so good as to take a glass up to the main truck and tell us what those sails are."

"Aye, aye, Sir!"

"And take Mr Woakes with you. It will aid in his education."

The two boys grinned at each other as there was nothing more than a midshipman loved than climbing around in the rigging.

"And no skylarking," growled McGivern.

The boys grabbed telescopes and ran up the ratlines like a pair of monkeys, shunning the lubber hole in the futtock shrouds by hanging on by their fingers and toes, and passed the lookout to the royal yard where they could stand, heads level, with the truck.

"Scan the horizon first," Quinten said.

As they stood either side of the mast, they did not impede each other in any way.

"Did you see any sails?"

"Only the ones to the south," Peter replied.

"Check the northwest quadrant again."

Peter did and stopped to focus on something.

"There's sails there on the horizon."

"How would you describe them?"

"Triangular?"

"Lateen, now look at the ones to the south."

He focussed his telescope and watched them for a minute or so."

"Tell me what you see," Quinten said,

"Lateen sails, two sets, coming towards us."

"What direction are the ones from the north going?"

He swung his telescope around to find them.

"Towards us as well."

"Now tell the captain. Be accurate and succinct. Take a stay to the deck, I will stay here."

Wolfgang had watched the whole exchange and smiled when he saw Woakes coming down the stay hand over hand.

"Well, Mr Woakes, what have you to report?" he said as the boy stood at attention in front of him.

Two sails to the south, both lateen rigged heading this way. A further two sails two points off the port bow also heading towards us."

"Could you make an estimation of their closing speed?"

"No, Sir. I believe that is what Quinten, I mean, Mr Stirling is doing now, Sir."

"Get back up there and report when you can."

"Aye, aye, Sir."

Wolfgang turned to his first.

"Madagascar pirates, you think?"

"Aye, I would think so. Nothing we can't take care of if we need to."

They sailed on seemingly unconcerned, then there was a hail.

"Deck there," Stirling called down. "There's a third ship joined the two to the south, a xebec if I'm not mistaken."

"That makes it more interesting," McGivern said.

"Closing at about three knots. About seventeen miles from the south. The ones off the bow are around fifteen miles off and closing at fifteen knots."

Marty joined them, having heard the hails in his cabin. "Something interesting happening?"

"A gaggle of Madagascar pirates if I'm not mistaken." Wolfgang smiled.

"They never learn, do they." Marty grinned wolfishly.

"How is your shoulder these days?" Wolfgang asked ingenuously. Marty had been shot in the shoulder by a Madagascar pirate some years ago.

"Aches when it's cold and damp. We won't give them the chance this time. Call the Pride up to hailing distance."

The sleek schooner came up to fifty feet off their beam.

"We can expect company in less than an hour. I would have you run as the Pride is faster than anything they have."

Captain Dunbar visibly bristled at that and shot back.

"We FIGHT."

Marty wasn't surprised at the response from the bristly captain. "Then stay to my lee side and be ready to repel boarders. I expect them to send two dhows after you and the xebec and two dhows after us." He grinned and doffed his hat.

"I think you offended him," Caroline said from behind his right shoulder.

Marty turned to tell her to go below but swallowed his words when he saw she was dressed for war and carrying her rifle, sword, and pistols.

Caroline heard what was going on from Matai and changed into a set of clothes she hadn't worn for a while. The leather bodice was a little tighter but as it was laced up that didn't matter. The riding trousers were normally worn under a riding habit and were held up with her tooled leather weapons belt.

She pulled on knee length leather boots that had a cavalry style flap over the knee to mid-thigh and soft leather soles to grip the deck. She stood up and Mary handed her the small sword from the selection in her carry case. She clipped the scabbard to the ring on the belt. Next, she selected a pair of Francotte revolvers from Marty's weapons case and attached them to the belt with the belt clips after carefully loading them. A long-bladed dagger with a basket hilt was slipped into a sheath at the back of her belt to be used as a main gauche. She donned a broad-brimmed hat with a jaunty feather in the band and collected her rifle and a shoulder bag of ammunition.

She examined herself in the mirror and nodded.

"That will do nicely."

Sam came in to collect Marty's weapons harness and gave a low whistle.

"Ma'am, you looks real warlike."

"Thank you, don't forget his rifle and ammunition."

Sam grinned showing shiny white teeth and gathered up Marty's Durs Egg Carbine and a bag of cartridges.

She went up on deck and heard the old hands telling the new hands that "Lady Caroline ain't no ordinary lady, she do fight beside his lordship." She smiled and took that as a compliment.

She walked up on to the quarterdeck and stood behind Marty who had just finished his shouted conversation with Captain Dunbar. He turned as she observed, "I think you offended him." He was about to say something but when he took in her dress and armaments, he swallowed it. She smiled sweetly.

Sam helped Marty into his weapons harness and handed him his rifle.

"Where's Adam?"

"On his way up top, said he wanted to get as high as he could," Sam said.

Marty looked up and saw him pass through the lubber's hole in the mainmast futtock shrouds. He carried on until he got to the main topsail yard where the ratlines stopped and there was a platform. He settled himself and Marty swore he saw him tie himself on.

"That's as high as he will get."

Taking their cue from the preparations on the quarterdeck many of the marines took their rifles and swivel guns up into the rigging. No order had been given but they had all heard the hails and the shouted exchange with the Pride. In fact, the whole crew quietly went to stations and settled down on the deck out of sight of any ships coming up on them.

"Do you think we might have overtrained them?" Marty grinned at Wolfgang.

"Why, Admiral, what a thing to suggest!" Wolfgang grinned back.

Hector appeared from below and trotted up beside Marty and sat by his left leg. Sam had put on his fighting collar that Marty's brother had made for Blaez to protect his neck. He looked at Marty expectantly.

"You'll get your chance," Marty said and patted his head. Hector had grown to a size that Marty didn't need to bend to pat his head as it came up almost to his waist.

"Deck there, the two ahead of us are swinging to parallel our course a mile off," Quinten shouted down.

"Come down and take your fighting station," Wolfgang called back up then turned to McGivern. "They will wait until the xebec takes us on. We look like a pair of merchantmen so they will split their force and try and take both ships. We will deal with the xebec and its consorts then go and aid the Pride."

"Understood, Sir."

"Have your men double shot the eighteens and load the fore carronades with smashers, the aft with cannister and small ball to rake their quarterdeck. We don't need to be encumbered with prizes or prisoners so shoot to sink them."

This was one of those moments that the SOF showed its ruthless side. Logic said the pirates would be hung if they were captured so they would save the hangman the trouble. The sharks would eat well.

"Ships on our stern have put on speed. Looks like they will be up to us in about twenty minutes. Take us to quarters quietly, Mr McGivern."

The thump of hammers was heard from below as the men removed the bulkheads that defined the captain's cabin. The passenger cabins were built into the forward hold and Orlop deck so didn't need to be taken down. They were now dark as the order went around to extinguish all lights and the occupants sat quietly waiting.

The ship was ready for war in no time. Caroline loaded her rifle and took position close to the stern rail. Marty was further forward with Hector, and the Shadows, without Adam, had taken their positions in a loose circle around them both.

She watched the xebec approach, it looked to be heading to come up on their port side. She knew enough about sailing to know that with the wind coming on their stern there was practically no wind gauge to make the decision for their captain. *Maybe the captain is right-handed,* she mused.

"No shooting until I give the command," Wolfgang warned.

As the xebec started to pass them just half a cable away their forward gun fired a shot across their stern. At the same time one of the dhows swung to starboard to come up the starboard side. They were only fifty feet away.

"You may fire as you bear," Wolfgang said.

Caroline had already picked her first target. She brought the rifle up and steadied her aim by holding a stay with the gun lying on her forearm. She fired.

On the dhow the rudder swung unmanned as the helmsman took her bullet in the chest. The boat veered with the wind away from the Unicorn just as the aft eighteens opened up. The veer didn't save the dhow as two of the large balls smashed through her side, tore through the mass of men and exited out the other side in a pink spray of blood and body parts. Caroline reloaded as the port battery took on the xebec which had come almost abeam of them. Gordon McGivern had waited until he could serve her a full broadside.

Behind her the carronades chuffed their loads of canister and small ball at the xebec's quarterdeck. At one hundred yards the effect of the well-aimed shots was devastating, levelling the steering gear and killing almost everyone. One man staggered around; half his face missing. Marty put him out of his misery. The main battery kept firing, aiming for the waterline. Both ships started to sink, the carronades killing swathes of men on their decks.

A grapnel hook flew over the stern rail followed by several more. The other dhow had evaded the stern chasers and made it up behind the Unicorn. Shouts came from below followed shortly by the sound of fighting.

Caroline was halfway through reloading when a head appeared at the rail. She dropped her rifle and pulled her pistols, cocking and firing the right one. The shot was a little wild but still clipped the man's head causing him to fall to the deck rather than land on his feet. Hector appeared and started savaging him.

She had no time to worry about that as more men reached the rail and were clambering on the deck. She started firing with both hands alternately. At such close range she could hardly miss. Then Antton was there on her right and Matai on her left. They also carried revolvers and the three of them laid down a hail of fire into the boarders.

Marty and Sam joined the party then Chin arrived, butterfly swords flashing. Sebastian and the other two embassy men were firing rifles for all they were worth on the main deck. Adam was picking the pirates off from the tops with the marines up there. Any boarders did not get much further than the rail and an impressive pile of bodies formed.

At the stern, once their pistols were empty, swords were drawn and when it was over the helmsman told his messmates,

"Lady Caroline fought like a veteran. Sword in one hand and dagger in the other, screaming like a banshee. Them pirates never knew what hit 'em. Then there was Hector. I seen him kill at least three men. That bloody dog is worse than his father."

What he didn't know was that Melissa and Mary killed four pirates that got past the men guarding the transom. Melissa shot one twice in the chest and then a second once through the heart. Mary shot one through the stomach then put a bullet in his head. Her second was a clean kill as the man attacked her with a raised sword, she shot him in the forehead as cool as you like.

Over on the Pride they had their own troubles to deal with. The two dhows that approached from the north were crammed full of men and were armed with twenty-four-pound bow chasers. The Pride's gunners got off two broadsides against one, but she did not have a big enough crew to fight both sides at the same time, so the second dhow got alongside relatively unscathed and men started to pour over the side.

The crew were fighting hand to hand and were gradually getting forced back. Every man including the servants took up arms and fought like the very devil. Men fell and their numbers were slowly diminishing. It was getting desperate.

Then the Unicorn arrived, her sharpshooters picking pirates off from behind before they got alongside with her marines, armed with pikes and bayonets, lining the rail ready to board.

Once they were alongside the undamaged dhow, the marines led by Captain Declan O'Driscol, attacked the pirate's rear, their pikes and bayonets doing fearsome damage. Wolfgang and the rest of the crew swarmed after them.

Marty and Caroline stayed on the Unicorn's quarterdeck and used their rifles when they could spot a clear target. Hector prowled the deck looking for any that might sneak across from the dhow.

"It's very nice having you here beside me, but don't you usually join your men?" Caroline asked Marty.

He fired his gun and a pirate fell from the Pride's rigging.

"I would but the mission in Burma is too important to risk me getting hurt."

Caroline smiled, maybe her husband was growing up at last.

Peace settled over the water, interrupted occasionally by a shot as someone took pity on a survivor in the water. All the pirate vessels had sunk or were sinking. The Great White had her fill and swam off leaving the rest for her white tip oceanic cousins and their smaller relatives to have their share.

The Unicorn's butcher's bill was two dead and five wounded. The Pride's was much worse.

"Seventeen dead and twenty wounded of which at least three won't live to see the sun rise tomorrow and another two will lose limbs." Shelby reported.

"Lord, I should have run," Dunbar said looking at the row of bodies laid out on the deck. He felt that his pride had caused their deaths.

Marty patted him on the shoulder, he had been told of how Dunbar had been in the forefront of the fighting.

"You survived and your ship is undamaged. Your men are stronger because of it and will be closer because of the shared experience. You are stronger because of it and the men will respect you even more because of your leadership. I will ask Wolfgang to send across replacements and a squad of marines so if this happens again you are better prepared."

The dead were buried at sea. They were saluted by a volley of rifle fire as their bodies were consigned to the deep. Marty read from Revelations, which the men approved of. Then they put on as much sail as they could and followed the wind east past the southern tips of India and Ceylon before turning northeast into the Bay of Bengal.

Any ship that came, or even looked to come, close was greeted by the sight of the Unicorn baring her teeth as she ran out her guns. It was enough to ensure a peaceful passage.

Marty had his regrets. He had intended for the encounter with the pirates to give the men some much needed practice. He should have been firmer with Dunbar and insisted he run. He wouldn't make the same mistake again.

A Cool Reception

They arrived in Yangon and discovered that the Irrawaddy River was navigable up to at least Pryay if not to Thayet. This was good news and allowed them to make accurate charts of the river system as they sailed. Sir Raymond, who spoke Burmese, searched for, and found a man who could act as a river pilot.

The first leg through the delta was the trickiest and by the time they got to the river proper the men were tired out from trimming and setting the sails, but the scenery was exquisite. The ladies especially spent the days gazing out at paddy fields with men and women up to their knees in water, bending over to tend the rice plants. Oxen and water buffalo wallowed or towed sledges and primitive ploughs.

The large ships certainly attracted attention and children would run along the riverbank shouting and waving. The pilot soon proved his worth, saving them from mud banks and shallows which the shallow draft river boats could often skim over. He was also quite the fisherman and soon had a line with a string of baited hooks running from the stern. By the end of the first day, he had caught a number of large snakehead fish. This obviously predatory fish had a mouth full of sharp teeth and their little friend whacked them on the head with a club as soon as they hit the deck.

That night Cetan, as they discovered he was called, worked with Roland to create a delicious fish curry. Marty was happy, especially as the next day Cetan bargained with a local fisherman for a basket of large, fresh water, tiger prawns.

The river ran pretty much due north once they passed Moyo and the crew had a much easier time of it as there were less shallows to be avoided and curves to be negotiated. They stopped at Thayet and Arnold questioned Cetan about the river from there on.

"He says that it is deep enough for a while but there are shallows with many sandbanks after that. He advises us to leave the ships here and take river boats," Sir Raymond translated.

They went ashore to hire riverboats to take them to Ava. A trader was found who had a pair of boats of the right size who was prepared to make the trip for an extortionately high price. Sebastian was convinced the trader had ideas of robbing and abandoning them and told Marty what he thought.

"We will distribute our marines and the Shadows across the boats for added security. Some overt cleaning of weapons should be enough to put those ideas to bed," Marty responded.

The boats, known as Knau, had high ornate sterns and a single mast seated about two thirds of the way towards the front of the boat which carried a pair of square sails. The boat could be sailed or rowed by eight pairs of oars by the sixteen-man crew. They were around sixty feet long by fifteen wide and made of teak. They normally carried rice from the rich delta area up to Pryay and from there to Thayet and Mandalay.

There was a long cabin that ran from the stern to amidships, the roof of which served as a kind of quarterdeck where the captain sat under a canvas shade to steer the boat using a tiller that operated a pair of steering oars. Inside there was a captain's cabin and a sleeping area for the crew as well as a simple galley. Marty had them build cabins and allocated one to the single ladies who shared, one for him and Caroline, one for the embassy officials who also shared, and one each for the married couples. The rest of the men slept either on deck or in the common area.

The Unicorn and Pride would stay in Thayet and would carry messages to the British ambassador in Calcutta. The Unicorn would also thin out any pirates she came across if she had the chance but there would be one ship in Thayet at all times.

It took four days to get organised and a large outlay of cash in the form of silver coins, but they were finally ready to move. The crews rowed their boats out into the stream and started upriver. Sails were hoisted and they bustled along at a good six knots. Marty had a man in the bow sounding as they went, and Sebastian kept himself busy by noting the readings and the river's course with his pocket compass. The captain of the boat thought this highly peculiar, but Marty was able to chart a fairly accurate record of the river that would turn out to be very useful in the coming years.

Now they had to make another two hundred and forty miles at around fifty to sixty miles a day if they were lucky. Marty thought it would take a week and had looked into going by cart, but that was even slower even if the route was more direct.

The miles ticked by and the shoreline became more hilly and less cultivated. They were three days out when they saw the first cavalry squad. The men rode to the bank and followed them for a while before one broke off and rode east.

"Do you think they know we are coming?" Sebastian grinned.

"Since we entered the river, I expect," Marty said.

"We need to establish exit routes if this all goes wrong," Sebastian said suddenly serious.

"Yes, I have had that in mind. I think we need to quietly acquire a couple of these boats and some horses."

"We have an agent or two here, one of which bought the residence. I will have a chat with them and see what we can do."

"Hmm. They are probably known to the powers that be, do we have anyone sleeping?"

Sebastian grinned again. Why, I do believe I may know of someone."

"Bloody spies," Marty laughed.

Ava came into view on the south bank. The first thing they all noticed was the fort.

"That is Hsin Gyone or Elephant Moat fort," Cetan said.

Marty scanned it with his pocket telescope noting the height of the earthworks and the number and types of cannons.

"Whoever designed it has never had to face a British warship. The earthworks are not high enough and the guns are not protected by caissons. Not only that but if I'm not mistaken those are piles of stone shot."

"No ovens?" Sam asked.

"No, so no worries about hot shot, and the guns are nine pounders if I'm not mistaken."

"They could still be a problem if we try to pass them in one of these boats," Sebastian said.

"Indeed, but a gun or bomb ketch could sail right up the river to her and beyond as could cutters full of soldiers."

Pagodas dotted the skyline. Ancient buildings with gold conical towers standing above brilliant white stone or yellow sandstone. They approached a landing, a lonely figure stood waiting for them. As they manoeuvred to dock, a squad of soldiers appeared and lined up smartly. They were armed with bows.

Marty told everyone to stay put and stepped ashore alone. He was dressed in full Admiral's uniform, his honours glinting in the sun. Sebastian stood at the gangplank, Sir Raymond and Peter De'ath behind him.

As Marty stepped ashore the individual stepped forward and introduced himself.

"Lord Martin, I am Chandra, your agent here in Ava."

By agent, Marty knew he meant land agent rather than secret agent. Chandra was an Indian from Assam, a territory the Burmese had wanted to acquire for a long time.

"Nice to meet you and who is this fine fellow coming out of the shadows?"

The fine fellow was a richly dressed Burmese. He wore an embroidered silk sarong over a white silk shirt, his head wrapped in a typical Burmese turban.

"That is the secretary to the first secretary to the minister for foreign affairs."

Marty noted the implied insult in the choice of person to greet him. As Ambassador he warranted a greeting from the minister himself.

"Really. Tell him when the minister is prepared to greet me in person, I will take up residence."

The 'fine fellow' strutted towards him. Marty turned and walked back to the boat causing a look of confusion to come over the 'fine fellow's' face. That was compounded when Chandra passed the message.

Marty kept his back turned to the man after he had gained the deck and was joined by his staff. He could hear the rapid-fire exchange behind him then the 'fine fellow' left. The soldiers stayed at attention in the sun.

Time passed and the sun got higher, Marty and his people sat drinking tea under a shade. The soldiers stood in the sun.

"I'm amazed one hasn't fainted by now," Sebastian said as he coolly watched them. "They have been at attention for over two hours now."

As he said it an officer appeared, and the men wheeled and marched away. Marty watched and waited. The sound of a large number of marching feet slowly got louder until a column of soldiers, three men wide, came into view.

"They sent a company," Sebastian noted professionally, "and this lot have muskets."

"A show of strength," Marty said.

The column performed a smart evolution to put them in two ranks. They smartly dressed their lines until they were parallel and evenly spaced then ported their arms.

A gilded sedan chair appeared, carried by four men, the sides closed by light material. Secretary to the first secretary trotted along beside it. It was placed gently on the ground and one of the bearers pulled back the cover.

Chandra laughed.

"It is the minister himself and he does not look happy. I need your full title and honours."

"Probably ripped from the arms of his mistress," Marty quipped and gave him the full nine yards.

Marty stepped up onto the gangplank and walked across to the shore then stopped. Sebastian stepped up on his right shoulder and Sir Raymond on his left. The three marched in step precisely halfway to the sedan chair and stopped. Chandra stood behind Marty within muttering range.

A rather large man was helped out of the chair by the secretary to the first secretary and adjusted his dress before walking with a dignified set of his head towards them, stopping six feet away and waiting while he was announced by the secretary to the etc, etc.

Marty bowed the precise amount required by protocol and it was returned by the minister. There was tension in the air. Chandra announced who Marty was.

"I have the pleasure to present Viscount Martin Stockley of Purbeck, Knight of the Bath, Rear Admiral in his Majesty King George the fourth's Navy and Ambassador to the kingdom of Burma." He stood back to translate.

"I welcome your Excellency the British Ambassador. Your presence is as surprising as it is welcome. We did not know they would send such an august person."

"I thank the foreign minister for his kind welcome. We did not want to embarrass him by being welcomed by a junior." Marty smiled as he landed the barb.

The minister was up to it.

"Very considerate. Are these your aids?"

"Yes. This is my military attaché, Lord Sebastian Ashley-Cooper Major of Rifles, and my chargé d'affaires, Sir Raymond Johnson."

"Most welcome, gentle sirs. Do you wish to inspect the honour guard?"

"I would be delighted." Marty knew this was an expected formality and kept pace with the minister as he waddled down the line. Marty was verbally impressed by the turnout and took the opportunity to get a close look at their weapons.

Well-kept Portuguese, flintlock muskets from the turn of the century. Swords have a long hilt but are not long enough to need it. No guard, curved blade about twenty-four inches long. Officers' swords are the same but more decorated.

The minister was speaking.

"These are men from the 1st Capital Defence Regiment and are all sons of landowners."

"They look well trained and very well turned out." Marty was not above polishing the man's obvious pride.

"They are the best."

Marty finished his inspection and walked the minister back to his chair.

"I have a gift. May I present it to the minister in thanks for his welcome?"

The minister looked surprised but nodded. Marty signalled and Adam, in full livery, stepped up from the boat carrying a fine French-made, rosewood chest. His progress was slow and refined.

Marty took the chest, and with a bow, handed it over. The minister took it, obviously restraining himself. He sat in his chair and opened the chest. His eyes widened and he reached inside and took out an exquisitely crafted, silver gilt figurine depicting the birth of Venus by John Bridge. She was bare chested and reclining on a small mountain of shells. He examined it and noticed that one shell had a hinge. He raised it and revealed a fine glass-lined compartment. It was an inkwell.

It was obviously an expensive gift, and the minister was very pleased and effusive with his thanks telling Marty if he needed anything all he had to do was message him. Marty was modest and assured him he would.

As soon as the minister departed, ox carts turned up to carry the household baggage and goods to the residence. Marty and Caroline were provided with a small carriage drawn by a single horse. It was four wheeled with large rear wheels and half-sized front wheels. It had no suspension.

While the temples and official buildings were made of stone the houses were made of wood and predominantly on stilts. The more salubrious were multi-story with ornate roofs. They followed the city wall around to the east. Their convoy and the marines marching in step attracted stares and children marched along beside them imitating their stride. Dogs paced them barking, "Stay boy," Marty said quietly to Hector as the dog took offence.

They stopped before an ornate gate that had a pagoda-like tower built on top of it.

"That's very grand," Caroline said.

Chandra's face was beaming.

"Oh, Lady Caroline, I am hoping you will enjoy the house that I have found you. Please."

He stepped down from the carriage and offered his hand. She winked at Marty and let Chandra help her out. Marty followed.

Chandra led them through the gates into an exotic garden. Several gardeners lined up beside the path to greet them. Marty stepped ahead of the party and nodded to each one as they passed. One stood slightly apart from the rest and was last in line. Marty recognised that he was the senior man and stopped to have a word.

"This is Myaing, the head gardener."

"Very pleased to meet you. The gardens are beautiful. You and your men do an excellent job."

Myaing stood proudly straight at the compliment and after the party had passed strutted away with his men showering him with compliments.

The house was three stories, made of teak and ornately carved. The ground floor was set above the ground on yard-long posts and steps led up the outside to the first floor which had a broad balcony. More steps led up to the third floor which was also surrounded by a balcony. On the south side the second-floor balcony extended out into a sun terrace that had ornate railings and was supported by stilts. The roof was pitched and tiled, and the eaves were carved with fantastic beasts.

"Where do we house our men?" Marty asked Chandra.

"There is another house behind this one, but it only has one floor."

"On stilts?"

"Oh yes, they are all on stilts in case the rivers flood."

It made sense.

"Get the men settled in the house behind this one and let me know when you are done. From the look of things, you will be able to have a room in here," Marty said to Declan.

He was right. There was plenty of room for everyone. He and Caroline had most of the second floor and their rooms led out onto the sun terrace. Melissa and the embassy staff got the remaining rooms on that floor. The Shadows and servants got the first floor and the ground floor was just for receiving guests and embassy business.

The marines got the bed up to their bedroom with much sweating and swearing. Their presence made official with a short ceremony that saw the union flag raised on a pole at the front. A bugler played reveille.

Roland installed himself in the kitchen and prepared a midday meal as Chandra had made sure they had fresh fruit and vegetables as well as meat.

The Boat Race

They were given the first day to settle in and then a messenger trotted up to the house with a summons for Marty to present himself to the king.

"At least he is prompt," Caroline said from where she was unpacking dresses with Tabetha.

"You had better get a move on. He wants to meet you as well." Marty looked smug as he and Adam had finished unpacking the day before, but then he didn't have four full ship's trunks of clothes plus accessories in a fifth trunk.

He had slept well and was ready for whatever the day brought. The house was designed such that the prevailing breeze blew through it on all levels, and it was cooler than their cabin on the Unicorn.

His weapons chest was open, and he was checking his guns and blades for rust. Adam was helping him and asked, "Will you require your uniform or a suit?"

"For the first meeting let's go with the uniform and all the shiny bits."

Caroline sighed.

"Something wrong, dearest?"

"I really do not know what to wear for a meeting with the king that I won't melt in."

Marty knew what she meant. His uniform was made of wool and designed for a northern climate. He would be suffering as well.

Dressed up to the nines the coach carried them to the royal palace. An overly ornate building, in Marty's opinion, with its carvings of animals and gods it was more like a temple than a palace. They pulled up at the front and were about to get out when the coach lurched, sending them back onto their seats. The driver was having a hard time keeping the horse in hand as it shied and skittered nervously.

Marty jumped out, went to its head, and held the bridle, speaking calming nonsense into its ear. The cause of the panic was obvious, a very large elephant with metal sheathed tusks, and a pair of soldiers mounted on its back was strolling past. It was indifferent to the horse and carriage giving Marty only a cursory glance. The horse on the other hand was frightened and Marty had to hold it firmly to stop it rearing.

Once the elephant had passed the horse settled down and Marty handed it back to the driver before helping Caroline dismount. Adam followed, carrying a long slim, highly polished rosewood box.

"You have horsehair and snot on your uniform," Adam said.

"Can't be helped, we don't have time to go back and change."

Marty took Caroline's arm and walked her towards the door. A servant appeared from nowhere, bowed and beckoned them to follow her. A short flight of steps took them to floor level and. as they passed through the door, Caroline gasped. The room inside was gilded from floor to ceiling.

Marty scanned the occupants; they were the only Europeans.

"Viscount Stockley?" a man with a European cast to his otherwise Burmese features and a decidedly English accent said, as he walked up to them.

Marty nodded.

"My name is George Gibson, and I will be your translator when you attend the king."

"Hello, George, pleased to meet you. This is my wife, Lady Caroline."

"You seem to have had a close encounter with a horse?"

"It spooked when it saw an elephant, I had to calm it."

"Flighty animal, let me get that sorted for you." George clapped his hands and a servant girl appeared. "Give her your coat, she will have it sorted in a trice."

Marty took off his coat and handed it to her. She rushed off after bowing.

"Would you like some refreshment while we wait for the king?"

"Yes please," Caroline said gratefully.

He clapped again and a tray of fruit juices was offered.

"How do you like our rather ostentatious audience room?" George asked with a sardonic smile on his lips.

"Impressive," Marty replied truthfully.

"We Burmese like our glittery things and our kings like them more than most."

His coat was returned spotless. Marty put it back on and checked the pockets. Everything was still there.

"Were you educated in England?" Caroline asked.

George smiled. "English father and Burmese mother. Educated at Winchester. Mother and I came back here when the old boy left this mortal coil ten years ago. I have been serving at court for the last five years."

A gong sounded and a servant girl took their glasses.

"The king approaches. You are the guests of honour this morning and will be presented first. "

Doors at the far end of the room opened and all the Burmese knelt on the floor abasing themselves, foreheads on their hands. Marty and Caroline bowed and curtsied respectively.

The king was slim, around five feet two inches tall, dressed in an ornate robe with heavily embroidered shoulder pads. He carried a sword with a gold and ivory inlaid hilt. His gaze took in the room and settled on the Stockley's.

He strutted up and stood, arms crossed, feet a shoulder-width apart, with a fierce look on his face. He signalled to George and said something. George stood and spoke, apparently introducing them. Marty stood erect from his bow and Caroline followed suit.

"The king wants to know why you do not kneel."

"Because no Englishman abases himself to any man including his king."

The king grunted at the reply then said some more.

"The king says that he has granted the British permission to have an ambassador on sufferance, in the hope that the border dispute can be solved."

"We thank his Majesty for the opportunity and would like to present him with a gift from His Majesty King George."

Marty beckoned to Adam who stepped forward with the box held across his arms. Marty took it and presented it to the king who gestured for George to take it. George had a servant, who stood head bowed, hold the box. He opened it, the king stepped forward at the sight of the magnificent gold and jewel-encrusted sabre and sheath that lay within.

He reached in and took the hilt in his hand to lift the sword out. It was made by Wilkinson of Sheffield of the finest steel. The forty-inch blade was etched and engraved; the hilt richly decorated. Marty knew the balance point was just four inches from the ricasso making it feel light.

The king swung it, then held it up so a shaft of sunlight glinted off the blade.

"A beautiful sword," George translated.

"I will tell his Majesty that you like it."

"You know him?"

"He is a friend as well as my king."

The king turned his attention to Caroline.

"Your wife is very beautiful. I have twelve at this time. They are all beautiful."

"Thank you, your Majesty. It is not our tradition to have more than one wife."

"One wife gets too arrogant. Thinks she can tell you what to do. If she knows she can be replaced as first wife she knows her place."

Marty dug his elbow in Caroline's ribs as she took a breath. The king didn't notice. "Do you like boat racing?"

"I am a sailor, your Majesty. I love all things to do with ships and boats."

"Then you must attend the boat racing as my guest in five days' time." And with that he turned away and moved on to the next person still carrying the sword.

Caroline spent the next two days with Melissa rearranging their wardrobes to bring all their light summer dresses to the fore and sourcing materials that could be used to make suitable dresses of light fabric. Burmese women tended toward a type of collarless blouse and sarongs. They often wore flowers in their hair for decoration. Their clothing suited the climate but was totally unsuitable for a European lady.

They settled on light linen and muslin blouses and skirts of the same material. Dresses were made in the high-waist style fashionable at the moment in London, with round, high, necklines as it seemed women covered up in Burma. Coloured silk slips protected their modesty and created a pretty effect as the colour showed through the thin outer fabric.

Marty reverted to the clothes he wore in India. Linen suits, silk shirts, shoes, cotton socks that covered him to the knee to protect against low-flying mosquitos. He wore a broad-brimmed hat to protect his head from the sun and did without a neck cloth preferring to have his shirt open at the neck.

Two days after they moved in, they had a visitor.

"A Mr Simeon to see you, Sir," Adam said and held out a silver platter with a card in the middle.

Marty took the card and read it.

A. J. Simeon Esq
Trader in Fine Spices

"Did he say what he wants?"

"No, but he looks flustered."

"Better send him in then."

The man when he entered was in his fifties at a guess, tanned, dressed in a linen suit that needed pressing and had sweat stains under the arms. He held his hat clutched in his hands.

"Mr Simeon, what can I do for you?"

"Thank you for seeing me, Mr Ambassador, Sir." He had a Yorkshire accent. "I am hoping you can help me with a small problem I have." He looked at Marty expectantly.

"That entirely depends on what your problem is."

"Well, Sir, you see it's my son. He has gone and got himself in a bit of bother you see." He stopped and waited again.

"No, I don't and will not if you do not explain what the problem is fully and concisely," Marty said, his impatience beginning to show.

Simeon looked abashed and his hat suffered a serious bout of ringing.

"It's a bit embarrassing you see. He is fifteen and has gone and got a native girl pregnant."

"Do her parents know?"

"Yes, they do. The father is demanding he wed the girl." He looked anguished. "He be too young for that, Sir."

Marty looked at the man unsympathetically.

"Do you have a native mistress?"

"I do, Sir, " he said with his eyes on the floor.

"Does the boy know about her?"

"He does, Sir."

"Then you only have yourself to blame."

"But can't you intervene with the king? He can order this not to happen."

"No, I cannot." Then Marty had a thought. "The girl isn't a royal princess, is she?"

"Oh, no, Sir. She is the daughter of a farmer."

Marty knew enough to know that in Burma, like Britain, landowners had status.

"How much land does he own?"

"Not too much. Only about fifty acres."

Marty knew that was actually a substantial holding in Burma.

"Well, I am afraid I cannot help you. You had better come to terms with the girl's father." He went back to the letter he had been reading before the interruption. Clearly dismissing him. Adam, who was still in the room, stepped forward, took Simeon by the arm and led him out.

As soon as he had gone Marty sat back in his chair and shook his head. "Is this what ambassadors have to deal with?"

Over the rest of the day people seemed to pop up at random. Some to greet him, others to ask for his advice or help and one who wanted money. At the end of the day Marty called Adam,

"Adam, ask the embassy staff to attend me."

The three came in, all had amused looks on their faces.

"I have just experienced a rather chaotic introduction to being an ambassador. From now this is how we will work.

I will be available for unscheduled visits only between ten and twelve in the morning, weekdays only, on a first come first served basis. All the visitors will be seen by Peter who will decide if their case warrants my personal attention or if Sir Raymond can handle their case.

We will lunch from twelve to two where we can, if necessary, entertain worthies. After that there will be another three hours when scheduled meetings can be held. If I am not available for any reason Sir Raymond will stand in my stead."

"What am I to do?" Sebastian said.

"You are a spy, go spy." Marty grinned.

The day of the boat races came all too quickly. A messenger from the palace arrived at ten in the morning and Marty, Caroline and the embassy staff were escorted to the conjunction of the Irrawaddy and Myitnge rivers. There they were placed in a large shady pavilion that was constructed of teak poles supporting a thatched roof. Marty knew that the Shadows were not far away, and they were protected.

Marty need not have worried as they shared the pavilion with the king's wives. All twelve of them, who sat in strict order of rank with Queen Nanmadaw Me Nu (the first) sat closest to them.

"My husband ask that I talk to you," she said in broken English to Caroline. "He say it will help my English."

Caroline was delighted. and the two were soon chatting away like old friends. George joined Marty.

"Morning, Milord Ambassador," George said as he sat cross-legged on the cushion beside Marty.

"Call me Martin when we are off duty."

"Thank you. Have you seen Burmese boat racing before?"

"The only Burmese boats I have seen are the ones on the river or the ones used by their freebooters."

"Then you are in for a treat. The first race is fifty-four-foot-long boats that are carved from a single tree. There is a steersman at the back with a steering oar and up to eighty rowers who stand in the boat and push it along with oars."

"Eighty? Good God, man, how do they stay in time?"

"That is all down to the front two rowers. They have white paddles where everyone else has the house colour of the boat on theirs. The king's boat is the red one, and the other colours represent the villages where the boat comes from," George informed him.

"Is the king onboard?" Marty asked.

"Not on this one. He is on the dragon boat which races later."

A drum echoed across the water and four boats painted in different colours passed in front of them. Marty was impressed, the rowers stood almost chest to back and all wore the colour that represented their boat.

"It is impressive."

"Wait until the race starts."

George was right. The race started with the wave of a flag and the men put their backs into it. The sight of eighty men moving in unison was something to behold as they tore down the river.

The boats were evenly matched and first one then another would get its nose in front. The pavilion cheered for the king's boat of course and it got its bow in front in the final quarter of the course. However, the blue boat put in a final surge twenty yards from the line and just pipped them. A section of the crowd on the bank went wild.

The boats in the next race were eighteen yards long, canoe-like, with eighteen rowers to a side and a man at the stern who steered. The course was a thousand yards long. The boats were brightly painted, and the men dressed likewise. They rowed facing forward in a kneeling position with leaf-shaped paddles. Marty looked for a red boat and picked out the king in the port bow position.

"The king rows? I expected him to steer," Marty said.

"The man in that position sets the stroke," George replied.

"The queen tells me that he is a very proficient rower," Caroline said.

"Sebastian, want to take a bet on who wins?" Marty said over his shoulder to where the men sat.

"A guinea on the king," Sebastian laughed.

"I will back the yellow boat. I like the cut of their jib," Marty said.

That set off a round of betting with Queen Nanmadaw betting Caroline that the king would win. The other queens joined in and there was an air of excitement in the pavilion as the flag was raised.

The flag dropped.

The king set a fast rate and the other boats matched it. Once they were up to speed, they set a more energy-conserving rate and all eight boats were within a prow's length of each other.

They were at the halfway marker and the yellow boat put in an extra effort to break away. The king seemed content to let them get a length ahead. Their rate slowed and the lead maintained.

At the two-hundred-yard marker the king dug in and increased his rate. The chase was on, but had he left it too late? The pavilion was on its feet, cheering and waving their arms.

The gap closed with every stroke. The yellow boat responded. It was neck and neck, the two boats swapping position with each stroke of the paddles.

A cannon fired as the boats passed the line. But who had won? They could not tell from the pavilion.

A flag was waved, and they strained to see what colour it was.

Red.

The king had won by the thickness of a plank.

Festival

It was the rainy season. It seemed to rain constantly, keeping everyone inside. It was tedious but at least Marty had a weekly audience with the king set up at his request. At these meetings the king would sometimes discuss sport, which he was very keen on. He wanted to know the various sports in Britain and told Marty of the different sports in Burma.

"One thing to look forward to is the Tazaungdaing Festival that marks the end of the rainy season," George told him before one such session. "It is linked with the Taunggy balloon festival and contests are held where villages compete at ox cart racing, boat racing, Chinlone (Cane Ball), Lethwei (boxing), Bando (defensive martial art) and Banshay (grappling)."

"Boxing?" Marty asked.

"Like bare-knuckle boxing but you can hit with any part of the body. Kicks, knees, fists, elbows and head. It is known as the sport of the nine limbs."

"Sounds brutal."

"It is. The more blood the more the crowd likes it." George laughed.

They were called into the audience chamber where the king sat on a raised throne. He had ordered the room to be cleared of other people except Marty, George and two guards that were always present. Once they were alone the king stepped down from the throne that was raised a good four feet above floor level.

"My Lord Martin," he addressed him in English and looked mighty proud of his effort.

"Your Majesty," Marty said and bowed deeply. "Your English is improving daily." Marty knew that George had been giving the king English lessons.

"Problem on the border."

Marty stood up. "Which border would that be, your Majesty?"

"One with Assam." The king gestured to George to continue and strutted up and down.

"It's all a bit fuzzy up there when it comes to exactly where the border is. Assam was annexed fifteen years ago and has been a problem province ever since. The British seem to be, shall we say, encouraging the locals to be rebellious. It would help relations if that were to stop."

"I see," Marty said frowning, "what does he want me to do?"

"Write to the East India Company and ask them to refrain from trying to subvert the king's rule."

"I can, but that alone may not make any difference. What I will do is write to the commissioners and the governor and send a copy to the Foreign Office in London."

George translated for the king who immediately stopped pacing and smiled broadly.

"Good! Festival in one month you come. My guest. Bring wife."

George grinned and spoke to the king with a bow.

"He says you can bring your staff as well, but they must sit with the lords."

"Thank you, your Majesty. We are honoured."

Sebastian knocked on Marty's office door and stepped inside.

"Good morning, Boss."

Marty was reading a letter and indicated for him to take a seat. When he finished, he signed it, blotted it, folded it into an envelope and sealed it with wax and his diplomatic seal.

"My monthly report."

Sebastian took an envelope from his pocket and placed it on top of Marty's letter.

"For Beth?"

"Yes, Turner forwards them."

Marty nodded.

"What do you have to report?"

"Our agents on the Siam border report that there is an uneasy truce between the belligerents down there.

"That's not what we want. Can we stir things up?"

"If I can borrow Chin and Roland, I can kill two birds with one stone."

"How so?"

"Chin can pass for a Siamese and Roland is French so I can make it look like the French are supporting the Siamese at the same time as using his explosives expertise to stir things up. We can also map the route and the terrain around it."

"What do you have in mind?"

"The Burmese have a large army encampment at the point where they border Siam and the French supported Kingdom of Luang Phrabang. If there was an incident there."

"It could trigger an outbreak of hostilities. I think we can live without Roland for a month or so."

"I will leave straight after the festival."

The festival started and like the boat race they were escorted to pavilions. Marty and Caroline were taken to the royal pavilion where the king, his queens, children, and most senior ministers abided. The royal pavilion was raised so it had a panoramic view of the festival and had the main arena directly in front of it. Dancers were performing a drum dance. The rhythms were complex and the moves elegant and controlled.

Marty noted that the general populous seemed to take a much more free-for-all approach to the festival as they milled around the other side of the arena.

The next sport on show was Chinlone. Groups of men formed circles with a man in the centre holding a woven rattan ball. The men in each of the circles walked slowly around the man in the middle. At the sound of a gong the men in the centre kicked the ball up in the air to a man in the circle who used his feet or knees to send it back.

"The idea is to keep the ball from touching the ground without using their hands. If it does, that team is eliminated. The team that lasts the longest wins. It is not really competitive and there is no prize for winning, only pride."

It was not only not competitive but rather tedious. The only people cheering were those that had a direct relationship with the teams. In spite of that it was somewhat elegant, and the rhythms established were akin to some kind of dance.

"It is time for the boxing," George said, when only one team was left.

A ring of thick rope was laid down in the arena directly in front of the king's pavilion. Two young men came into the ring, their hands wrapped in cloth. They wore loincloths but were otherwise naked.

"This is a bout between two men of equal weight. George explained. "They are the champions of their villages. The colours of their armbands differentiate them."

Blue and yellow armbands were clearly visible on their upper arms.

"What are the rules?" Caroline asked.

"It is called the sport of nine limbs. Hands, elbows, knees, feet and the head can all be used. The fight continues until one of the men cannot or does not want to carry on."

"So, no rules, just beat the other man senseless." Marty murmured to Caroline.

There was a referee who carried a baton which he held out between the two men. He withdrew it and the fight was on.

The two were cagey to start with, feeling each other out. Jabs and kicks were exchanged but little contact made. Then yellow tried a vicious roundhouse kick which, if connected, would have knocked blue into next week. However, his foot met thin air as the man ducked and charged to grapple his off-balance attacker. Blue wrapped his arms around him from behind and tried to lift him.

Yellow's head snapped back, connecting with Blue's forehead causing him to loosen his grip. Blue staggered back, blood running from a cut. The crowd howled.

Yellow moved in for the kill and was stopped dead by a knee to the gut followed by a wicked right cross that took him on the eyebrow. Now both were bleeding. Yellow took the time to shake his head and wipe the blood away from his eye.

That gave Blue time to recover his wits and the two faced off again. This time they both attacked with a will. Knees connected to ribs; punches flew. But the split eyebrow was the deciding factor as Yellow targeted it again and again. It was obvious that Blue had lost the sight in that eye.

A cracking uppercut ended the match. Blue hit the dirt and didn't get up.

"A good fight to warm up the crowd," George said. "Now we shall see the professionals."

"There are professionals?" Caroline was amazed that anyone would want to do it as a job.

"A boxer can work his way to being in the elite class and then he can enter professional bouts," George explained. "The last two were the amateur champions for their weight."

"These two are bigger," Carline said as two more men entered the ring.

"There is a lot of betting going on," Marty observed.

"It is a part of the entertainment."

The king said something to George who turned to Marty.

"The king wants to know if you would like to make a bet on who will win this fight."

The king's boxer won, costing Marty three guineas. He managed to perform a suplex, which knocked the wind out of his opponent, then followed up with an elbow to the temple which felled the man.

More bouts followed, some short and sharp others long and drawn out. George was excited.

"This is the final bout. An open contest with no weight limitation. A contest between the heavyweight champion and a Chinaman who has challenged him. It should be the highlight of the competition."

The two boxers that walked out were vastly different, one was large even by European standards and could probably match Sam in height and weight. Then Marty did a double take,

"What the hell! That's Chin isn't it?"

Caroline too had recognised the Shadow.

"Did he tell you he was doing this?"

"No, he bloody didn't, or I would have forbidden it."

Then Marty looked across at the second pavilion where his embassy staff was sitting and saw Sebastian grinning broadly at him. *What the hell are you up to?*

"I bet on the big man." The king leant towards Marty as he said it.

"I will take that bet," Marty said and held up his purse. "Twenty-five gold." He passed it to George.

The king nodded. The fighters were abasing themselves on the ground facing the king who waved a hand to signal the start of the fight.

They faced off and the referee raised his baton.

The big man bulled forward but Chin danced backwards, circling to keep inside the ring. He darted in and landed stinging blows to the head and chest of his opponent. The big man roared and swung a haymaker. Chin ducked under it and hit him in the abdomen. Marty heard the smack from where he was sitting.

Chin had made a mistake; the big man wrapped his arms around him and got him in a bearhug. He squeezed and you could see the strain in Chin's face.

Marty held his breath.

Chin had his arms free and slapped his cupped hands over the big man's ears then headbutted him on the bridge of the nose.

"That hurt," Marty said.

The big man let him go.

Chin danced away and did a couple of stretches. Marty could imagine the sound of pops as his spine realigned.

The big man had blood running from his nose and one ear.

"He broke his eardrum," Caroline said.

"And his nose. It's definitely not in line anymore," George said.

Chin recovered first, his opponent still dazed. He stepped forward nimbly and spun, leaping into the air, right leg extended. The heel of his foot contacted the temple and the man went down.

Chin stepped back thinking it was over, but the man, whose name was Nwarr (Bull), sat up. His eyes glazed. He shook his head to clear it.

He stood.

The crowd roared.

Damn, but he is tough.

Chin bowed to him in respect.

Nwarr bowed back and grinned showing missing teeth.

This time he was more cautious and kept his guard up. He started to move his feet keeping Chin more where he wanted him. Chin concentrated on staying out of reach.

Nwarr tried a couple of kicks which Chin blocked easily. He was actually more agile than Chin had given him credit for. On the other hand, Nwarr now knew he was up against someone who was skilled in the martial arts, not just some Chinese opportunist.

It became a contest between two styles, Chin's Kung Fu Wushu and Nwarr's knowledge of Lethwei, Bando, and Banshay.

Chin switched style. He had been fighting in the southern style which concentrated on punches and the rare kick but now went to Ying Zhao Pai (the Eagle Claw) style which included Chin Na (a form of grappling).

The change in stance and movement was immediately noticed by Nwarr and caused him to hesitate for just a second. Chin moved and Nwarr reacted a fraction too slowly, his punch grazed Chin's eyebrow. Chin's blow, however, hit home. A straight-fingered jab to the Rugen pressure point in Nwarr's right pectoral, followed by a leg sweep that took the big man down.

The jab to the pectoral caused a lot of pain and temporary paralysis, meaning Nwarr was slow to get up. Chin moved fast, spinning on the ground while using his core strength to rise up and deliver an elbow strike to the head.

Again, this was not enough to finish the big man off and Chin found his arm was numb from the hit. Nwarr got up swinging and connected at least twice, splitting Chin's cheek in the process.

Chin retreated, moving his arm to restore the movement. Nwarr pressed his advantage, crowding him and using his knees and fists to good effect. Chin broke away and retreated, the crowd booed.

He bounced on the balls of his feet and shaped like an English bare-knuckle fighter. His hands were fast jabbing with his left and attempting a stinging right cross that Nwarr dodged just in time. Nwarr pushed him away and tried a cross of his own. Chin dodged the fist but the following elbow hit his cheek. Blood flowed freely.

In the pavilion it was pandemonium. The king cheered and jumped up and down every time his champion made contact. Marty and Caroline cheered Chin on, standing and gesticulating.

Chin collected his chi and focussed. If he couldn't knock the big man out, he would have to try something else. He covered up his head and let Nwarr come to him. The big man threw punches and knee strikes. He moved in close and reached out to grapple Chin for a headbutt. Chin dropped his right arm, so his fist was just three inches from Nwarr's sternum.

He struck with all his chi focussed behind the strike. The effect was devastating. Nwarr's whole body seemed to vibrate from the impact and there was a loud crack. His feet left the floor, and he flew backwards for a foot before landing on his back on the ground.

He did not move.

The crowd was silent.

The referee knelt beside him and checked for a pulse. Grim faced he stood and gestured to Chin. He had won. But at what cost? Chin knelt beside Nwarr, checked his pulse, and ran his hands over the point of contact. There was a broken rib. He manipulated it gently into line then looked at Nwarr's face. His eyes opened and he took a long shuddering breath, winced, then looked at Chin.

Chin stood and held out his hand. The big man took it and allowed Chin to help him up.

The crowd cheered and cheered as the two men turned and bowed to the king.

That evening the Taunggy balloon festival took place. The king kicked it off by releasing a massive paper balloon that was richly decorated and powered by an oil burner suspended in the opening. That set off a wave of balloons that rose into the evening sky like so many fireflies.

Marty and Caroline were each provided with elaborately decorated balloons and released them simultaneously in a romantic gesture of togetherness. The balloons rose side by side as if connected. An auspicious sign according to the king.

Incident at Khote Wa

Sebastian, a patched-up Chin, Roland and one of their agents, known as Falcon, sat in the main room of the safe house that had been set up through their agent. They were going over the equipment and stores they needed to get to the golden triangle.

The border region where Burma, Siam and Luang Phrabang met had a growing reputation as a centre for opium growing. Hence the nickname of the golden triangle. Opium fetched a high price in China and in Europe and the fact that the area was right on the mighty Mekong River made transporting it easy.

Marty had talked with Sebastian and found out that he had asked Chin to challenge the champion to establish a cover identity for their travels. Sebastian and Roland would be Chin's support team as the man who beat the Bull toured across Burma.

Both Sebastian and Roland changed their appearances. Sebastian dyed his hair a dark brown and Roland shaved off the beard he had been cultivating for the last three years.

"Are you happy with the powder, Roland?" Sebastian asked.

"Oui, it is a little course, but it will suffice. The sulphur cakes are easy to pack, and we can source oil when we get there."

They had a small cart pulled by a pony that would carry their packs and trade goods, but most of the trip would be on foot and take about eight days.

They set off before dawn. Marty sent out the rest of the Shadows to make sure the area was clear of watchers, so they moved quickly to clear the town and get out into the open country. The roads were still a little muddy but were drying out fast now the rainy season was over. As the sun came up, steam rose from the ground and the humidity went up.

"I don't think I've ever sweated so much. My clothes are wet to my skin," Roland complained.

"It is pretty humid." Sebastian mopped his brow for the third time in as many minutes.

"It will get better later." Falcon grinned. He was half Burmese half Indian and was coping better than the Europeans.

He was right by ten o'clock it was just hot, they still sweated but it evaporated as fast as it formed. Because they were wearing boots and sweat had run down their legs and pooled inside them, Roland and Sebastian started to get blisters. Chin and Falcon on the other hand wore sandals and were not suffering.

At the first opportunity Sebastian bought sandals from an itinerant trader they passed on the road. He looked at their feet when they removed their boots and stockings. there were large blisters on the heels and the side of their big toes.

"He says he has a lotion that will fix them," Falcon translated.

The lotion was a mixture of some kind of alcohol and coconut oil that soothed the soreness. The blisters were lanced, the lotion applied, and feet bound in cloth. Falcon bargained with the trader and trade goods in the form of cheap knives changed hands.

The next problem they encountered was chafe. There were certain areas where sweat pooled and their clothes rubbed. They tried the same lotion and were pleasantly surprised that it worked. Falcon suggested they change into Burmese clothes, but they were unwilling to give up their trousers for what they saw as a skirt, but it came to a point where the chafe was bad enough to force them into it.

Sebastian was used to marching long distances being a soldier, but Roland was a cook and a sailor. He ended up in the cart as he couldn't keep up. Chin was stoic and if he was suffering didn't show it.

They reached their first overnight stop and put their cover story into play. Falcon loudly announced to the villagers that the man who had beaten the Bull at the festival was there to show his skills and take on any challengers.

Chin went through a shadow boxing routine which loosened his muscles from the day's walking and showed off some of his skills.

A crowd gathered as this kind of entertainment was rare and they had all heard about the fight as some had attended the festival and brought the story home. In fact, the details of the festival were travelling ahead of them as people went home and shared their stories. It was like the ripples from a stone dropped in a pool radiating out from Ava.

Children imitated Chin and the locals oohed and aahed until one man stepped forward to challenge him. The local champion, who was a match for weight and size.

The contest was short and sharp, Chin gave him respect and didn't toy with him. The blow that felled him came just three minutes into the bout. Their reward was to be fed and given a place to sleep. They also traded goods for coconut oil.

This was repeated until they were far enough from Ava to go incognito and to detour south into Siam for the final day's march to the golden triangle area. Now Sebastian and Roland disguised themselves as locals and they kept their distance from anyone they encountered on the road.

They knew they were entering the area as fields that would normally be planted with food crops were planted with poppies in various stages of growth. Some were at the seed pod stage and ranks of women were moving through the field, scoring the unripe seed pods with a multi-bladed tool. Others used a curved knife to scrape the dried resin from the pods.

As they passed through the area the presence of armed patrols increased. Some were soldiers but others looked more like bandits or militia. Either way they avoided them, keeping as low a profile as possible.

The River Ruak was the border between Siam and Burma. They found a campsite that was hidden from the road that ran along it and the patrols on the other side in Burma.

Once they were settled Roland began preparations. He ground up the tablets of sulphur to a powder and mixed that with the coconut oil and some naphtha that he had brought with him. He filled rough clay pots with the mixture and sealed them with softwood bungs. Then he measured out charges of gunpowder which were placed in bags that were carefully sewn up with a length of fuse through the seam. These were placed in the bottom of bowls made of much harder material than the pots which were placed on top. The bowls were chosen because their internal diameter was such that the pots were a tight fit. However, as they were hand made a certain amount of juggling went on to find good matches and the pots were tied in place with strong twine.

When all was ready Chin and Sebastian stole a boat and, in the dead of night, the three of them crossed the river into Burma. The poppy fields and drying areas were laid out before them. By the light of the moon, they slunk through the fields until they found several standing poppies. Roland placed a row of pots down the middle of each field spaced out fifty feet apart and ran a length of fast fuse along the row which he tied to the fuses in the pots.

They covered two large fields like this and placed individual pots in the middle of the drying and preparation sheds.

"Are we ready?" Sebastian asked.

"Oui."

The three stripped off the black coveralls they had worn. Sebastian and Chin were dressed in what looked like Siamese military dress and Roland in the uniform of a French infantry man.

Roland lit the fuses. Now came the tricky part.

The light from the burning fuses attracted the attention of the guards who immediately spotted the three men silhouetted against the glow.

The alarm was sounded.

The three of them retreated in orderly fashion and shot any guard that got close to the burning fast fuse. Roland shouting meaningless orders in French. The first charge went up followed by the rest at five-second intervals. Great plumes of fire lit up the sky and fire rained down on the fields. Then the charges in the sheds went up. The area was an inferno.

They made sure they were clearly visible as they retreated to the boat, trusting that any guards with muskets would be bad shots. Unfortunately, some were good shots with bows.

An arrow hit Roland in the shoulder. He staggered and dropped his French army issue musket. Sebastian grabbed him and hustled him into the boat while Chin covered them.

Once back in Siam they fired a couple of last shots at the guards on the opposite bank of the river before disappearing into the dark. At the camp Sebastian held a shuttered lamp while Chin attended to Roland's shoulder.

"It's barbed, we are going to have to push it through," Chin said.

He cut the uniform off to expose the entry point and by feel had established it was in a spot with no bone in the way.

"Get on with it," Roland growled through gritted teeth.

Chin ran his knife around the arrow shaft six inches from the wound and broke it off. He then cut a groove in the shaft protruding from Roland's shoulder.

"Need to cauterise it as well."

Roland rolled his eyes and put the end of a leather belt between his teeth.

Chin took a flask of priming powder and trickled a line of powder into the groove. He lit a slow match and handed it to Sebastian, then placed the side of one of his butterfly swords against the end of the shaft. In his other hand he held a rock.

"Ready?"

Roland and Sebastian both nodded.

"3, 2, 1."

Sebastian touched off the powder and a fraction of a second later Chin slammed the rock into the sword blade. The flash of light from the burning powder was extinguished as the shaft went into his flesh.

Roland stiffened, his eyes wide. Sebastian expected him to faint, but he stayed with them. Chin went behind him and grabbed the now exposed arrowhead and pulled the shaft out.

"One more thing to do then I will bind it up."

Roland knew what was coming and braced again as Chin poured neat alcohol into the wound to sterilise it. After that was done, he packed it with clean linen strips, and bound it with a bandage.

"Let's get out of here," Roland groaned.

Resuming their former disguises, they headed back the way they had come. The road was busy as troops marched along it towards the river. Falcon asked a soldier what was going on and was told the Burmese had made an incursion into Siamese territory.

"Is the war back on?"

"It never stopped."

As the army was one of the main benefactors of the opium trade the commanders were angry at the enormous loss of revenue caused by the fires that had spread across many more fields, effectively destroying the crop. Their response was to retaliate. Behind them Burmese troops had crossed the river bent on revenge.

"There is a lot of smoke behind us," Roland said from his perch on top of the wagon.

"Perfect," Sebastian said without looking back.

That evening in a comfortable hostelry on the Siam side of the river. Chin boiled used linen strips in water to sterilise and clean them and drizzled raw alcohol on some that he had ready to be used.

He examined Roland's wound closely.

"It is pink and healthy,"

He repacked it with the linen strips, dusted it with sulphur and rebound it with a clean bandage.

Falcon looked on curiously. He had not seen arrow wounds treated this way before.

Chin explained. "We need to keep it clean, or the rot will set in. The alcohol and sulphur help with that. The packing is to make sure it heals from the inside out. Otherwise, we leave a hole that can go rotten."

"Is that Chinese medicine?"

"The Europeans are learning how to treat wounds just a few hundred years late."

"Be nice Chin," Roland said. "Us poor primitives had a lot of catching up to do."

"You are a brave man. Most would have passed out from the treatment," Falcon told him.

"Not brave, stupid and stubborn. Sensible man would have," Chin said with a completely inscrutable expression as he tied off the bandage.

"Then you would have had to carry me."

"True, you are fat and heavy."

The banter continued until they slept.

In the morning they crossed back into Burma. The crossing was manned by guards, they found that the Burmese guards at the fields had blown up the story to where a division of Siamese troops and French soldiers had crossed the river and burnt the poppy fields.

Roland got a temperature and the wound reddened. Chin visited the medicine woman at the next village and got some herbs. "Jin yin hua and Huang qi to take the heat out of the wound and get rid of poisons." He boiled the herbs in water and then boiled the resulting liquor down to concentrate it. He soaked the linen strips in it and also made Roland drink some. The infection reduced over the next five days by which time they were a day away from home.

"You stirred up a hornet's nest," Marty told them when they finally got back to the residence. "The borders with Siam and Luang Phrabang have destabilised, and all sides are raiding back and forth. I expect the French to send an envoy here to assure the king that they had no part in it."

"Do you want him to have an accident?"

"Not yet. Let's see what he has to say first."

The French Envoy

Cyril Du Sept Fontaines, Envoy of the French Government was a colonialist of the first order. He worked tirelessly to expand French interests in Indochina and had ambitions to be the governor of all of Vietnam, Cambodia and what would come to be known as Laos.

He sat sedately in a canvas chair on the deck of the Corvette Cygne that was carrying him up the Irrawaddy River and watched the paddy fields pass by. The trip, so far, had been uneventful and had given him lots of time to ponder the recent events.

Somehow the Burmese had gotten the idea that the French were either behind or supporting the recent attacks on their poppy fields in the golden triangle. He had also heard that there was a new British ambassador in Ava. He wondered who it was.

Cyril was a former Major of Grenadiers and had fought at Waterloo and before that in Spain. He had a lot of respect for the British soldier and envied the level of training they had. It was that which he thought had won them the war.

His thoughts were disturbed by a lookout.

"Sail on the river ahead, three-masted ship, topsails set."

The captain looked perplexed and sent an aspirant up to try and identify it.

"A French-built frigate, flying British colours," the boy panted as he regained the quarterdeck.

"A capture from during the war," the captain growled.

The ship came into view around the bend ahead of them, she had topsails set and was making enough headway to maintain control over the current.

The two ships had ample room to pass as long as they stayed to their side of the channel. The British ship did just that and as she passed the captain growled again.

"The Unicorn, she was captured in Cartagena when she was named La Licorne. I was an aspirant then and on shore leave when they cut her out."

The captain of the British ship was on his quarterdeck and politely raised his hat in salute as they passed.

The French captain raised his hat in return. "Cocky bastard."

"What is a British frigate doing this far up the Irrawaddy?"

"You can ask them when you get to Ava."

They arrived in Thayet and were even more surprised to see an elegant American-made clipper flying the British Flag moored at the dock.

"The Pride of Purbeck," Cyril read and alarm bells started to ring in his mind.

"Can you find out who's ship that is, Frederic?" he asked his assistant.

Frederic was a member of the French Secret Service and attached to him to carry out those tasks that needed doing quietly. It wouldn't take him long to learn everything about the owner. In fact, it took longer than he expected, and Cyril was pacing up and down impatiently when he arrived back.

"Well?" he said before Frederic had a chance to say anything.

"She is the personal ship of Viscount Stockley who is the British ambassador. The frigate is also under his command and is heading to Calcutta. I was told that one of them is here at all times."

"Stockley?"

"Yes, Sir, is that significant?"

"I'll say it is! He was that devil Wellington's chief of intelligence in Spain and was at Waterloo. My Grenadiers faced him at La Haye Sainte along with the King's German Legion."

"I know him now; he took the emperor to St Helena and is rumoured to be in British Intelligence."

"And he is now Ambassador to the Court of the King of Burma. That is not good. We must be on our guard. He is not above killing anyone who gets in his way."

When they arrived in Ava, they found that the house they had been given to stay in was next to the British Residence. Cyril suspected that Stockley had had something to do with that. In fact, he hadn't; the king's minister who looked after these things just found it convenient to put all foreign diplomats in the same area.

He was also not surprised to find he would have to wait several days to see the king. The French were not a trusted country in these parts any more than the British and he wondered how they had finagled an ambassadorial presence here when the French had constantly been denied.

What did surprise him was an invitation to tea from Lady Stockley.

Caroline sat on the camomile lawn in the gardens of the residence with Melissa under a parasol. The two were elegantly dressed and wore fashionable hats rather than bonnets. Cyril was brought around the house to the garden when he encountered the guard in marine uniform at the gate. A whistled signal had brought a footman from the house who escorted him through the colourful and scented tropical garden to where the ladies sat decorously waiting to have tea.

He was surprised that there didn't seem to be more guards on duty. He only saw native gardeners trimming bushes.

"Monsieur Du Sept Fontaines, Milady," the footman said in a monotone.

Caroline treated him to a dazzling smile and greeted him in perfect Parisian-accented French.

"Good day, Sir. I hope you are in good health after your journey?"

"Lady Stockley, good morning. I am very well, thank you, and delighted to be in your company." Cyril bowed over her raised hand. "And this is?" he asked, shifting his attention to Melissa.

"My son's fiancée and my ward, Melissa Crownbridge."

He repeated the bow over Melissa's hand.

"Your son is here?"

"No, I am afraid not. He is serving in the Mediterranean on his ship."

"Aah, the demands of the service."

"Please sit and join us for tea."

A dark-skinned maid brought out a tray with tea followed by a footman with a tray of sweet delights.

"Thank you, Tabatha," Caroline said.

"I was surprised to receive your invitation, Lady Caroline."

"Please, here in the garden, let us dispense with formality. Call me Caroline. Why were you surprised? We are not enemies anymore."

"Then you must call me Cyril. No, we are not enemies, but we are competitors."

"Pft, that can be managed in a civilised manner."

"I saw that you have two ships at your disposal."

Caroline lifted the lid of the teapot to check the brew.

"How do you take your tea?"

"With lemon, if you please. No sugar."

Caroline poured, the ceremony of serving tea taking precedence over talking. She delicately placed a slice of lemon in his cup with a pair of tongs. Melissa placed a tea plate in front of him and asked, "Would you like a cake?"

"Thank you, a small one." He noticed the tea set was of the finest English bone china and decorated with the Stockley family crest.

There was still an empty chair,

"Will your husband join us?"

"He is busy with an unexpected petitioner. He will join us as soon as he can. You asked about the ships. The Pride of Purbeck is our personal yacht, the Unicorn is my husband's flagship."

"Ahh, yes, he is an admiral now, I remember seeing it in the Gazette."

"Only a rear admiral. Pleased to meet you, Monsieur Du Sept Fontaines," Marty said, as he walked across the lawn to join them.

Cyril rose and bobbed a bow, Marty held out his hand and they shook.

"Monsieur, Ambassador."

"Martin please. We are informal here in the garden in private." He sat and Carline served him a cup of tea. He took a cake.

Cyril noted that Martin, like his wife, dressed in the latest fashion of trousers rather than breeches and an open-neck shirt with no neck cloth. Marty took off his coat and handed it to a footman.

"Too hot for that out here. Please feel free to take off your coat."

Cyril had to decline as he was wearing a pistol under it.

Marty smiled at him knowing why. He had taken his fighting knife off his belt just before coming out and it was now carried by Henry, the footman in attendance.

"We were just talking about the Unicorn," Caroline said.

"On her way to India with dispatches. Did you see her on the river?" Marty said.

"Yes, we passed her. She is a very fine ship. French built?"

"Yes, I believe she is," Marty said, then abruptly changed the subject.

"I suppose you are here to reassure the king that the French had nothing to do with the debacle in the triangle. I told him it was bunkum. I mean, why would you do that?"

"You see the king often?"

"A couple of times a week." Marty tossed out as he reached for another cake. "Unfortunately, paranoia runs deep in the court. He has never trusted the French, or the British, come to that."

"Why did he allow you to be resident then?"

"Because he wants something. Assam to be exact. He does not want us to take it back and thinks that we are less likely to if we have diplomatic ties."

"A dangerous position to be in if he changes his mind or the East India Company decides it wants that land."

Marty shrugged, "I've been in worse places."

"The peninsula?"

"You were there?"

"And Waterloo."

"Your Hussars nearly got me in Portugal."

Cyril laughed. "You escaped by the skin of your teeth according to them. The ones that came back that is."

Marty reflected. "They were rash. If they had used more strategy, they could easily have won. As it was, my marines shot them to pieces."

"I suspected as much. You met the emperor."

"I did, more than once. He almost had me killed at one point in Paris."

"In Paris?"

"Yes, in his private rooms."

"My God!"

"I remember he said something like that when we escaped." Marty chuckled. "All things considered, I quite liked him as a man."

Cyril shook his head, not sure what to make of this quiet, ordinary man. He decided to be bold.

"Did you initiate the incident?"

"Now Cyril, we were getting along so well. If I told you I did, do you think you would leave here alive?"

The look in his eyes sent a shudder down his spine. This was a very dangerous man.

"I suppose not."

Marty laughed. "Well lucky for you I did not."

"Will you honour us by joining us for dinner?" Caroline asked. "Our chef is French and is amazing."

The food was cordon bleu. As good as the best in France, "Can I meet your chef?"

"Only if you promise not to steal him."

Cyril smiled as he ate the last mouthful of the pastry.

"That is unfortunately a promise I cannot give."

They introduced him to Roland anyway.

"You should open a restaurant in Paris," Cyril said.

"I did, in 1815, but only for a month or two."

Marty chipped in, "It was a roaring success. All of Napoleon's staff ate there. It was in the Rue de Miromesnil. I was the maître d'hôtel. "

Cyril suddenly realised what was being said. Stockley had actually opened a restaurant in the centre of Paris to spy on Napoleon's staff. That was not only audacious but damned brilliant. It was at that moment he understood he was out of his depth.

They sat and chatted over an exceptionally good Armagnac until around ten when Cyril said it was time for him to go.

"You are unfamiliar with the grounds, allow me to have one of my people escort you," Marty said.

He rang a bell and his manservant appeared.

"Adam, would you be so kind as to ask Sam to escort Monsieur du Sept Fontaine to his residence."

"Of course, Sir." Adam bowed and left. Five minutes later Sam arrived.

"Sam is my cox, he will escort you."

Cyril took in the massive bulk of the former slave noting the lack of fat over the rippling muscles as he moved. He also noted the almost machete-sized knife in a sheath on his hip.

"Take a lantern so Cyril doesn't trip."

"You are most solicitous, thank you."

"We wouldn't want you to have an accident would we."

If I did it would be at your initiation, Cyril thought.

Cyril finally got to see the king a week and a half after he arrived. He had no idea what was going on down on the border. He was met by George who acted as his interpreter as he spoke French as well as English and Burmese.

The king sat on his elevated throne some eight feet above the floor.

"I bring the greetings and felicitations from the golden throne of his Majesty King Louis the eighteenth of France to his most glorious brother the exquisite King Bagyidaw."

The king's reply was short, but George said, "The king returns the greetings of King Louis and wishes him well in return."

Cyril was sure that is not what the king said but ignored it and carried on.

"I am here as his envoy—" George interrupted him.

"Please wait for the king to ask."

The king was glaring down at him.

"Why do the French support the incursions onto our territory and destruction of our property?"

"Your Majesty, I am here to assure you that my nation has had no part in any military actions against your country."

The king barked a command, and a servant came in and placed a box on the floor in front of him. A second servant brought in a musket.

"Kindly explain what these are?"

Cyril knew immediately that the musket was a French Charleville that was used by the infantry. It was a flintlock.

"That is a Charleville musket, may I pick it up?"

He picked it up and examined it.

"This one is a 1766 pattern and according to the serial number was probably exported to America in support of their war of independence. Fifty thousand were manufactured and at the end of the war many were destroyed or sold off."

"You are very knowledgeable."

"I am a former major of grenadiers, Your Majesty."

The king gestured to the box. Cyril opened it. Inside was a uniform coat.

"This is a uniform coat of the 9th Light Infantry that was disbanded in 1815. Someone has attempted to," he was about to say 'deceive' but decided that implied the king was gullible, "plant incriminating evidence to imply that the French were involved."

The king took the offered route back to detente,

"Why would someone want to do that?"

"To discredit the French and make it seem that we have ambitions on your kingdom."

The king knew damn well they did and took time to think through how to balance the dual threats of the British and French. He had an idea.

"I will think on this. Please stay available."

He was dismissed.

Marty was summoned. He too was presented with the evidence.

"Do you know what that is?" He was handed the musket.

"French Charleville musket 1766 pattern. I have fought against the French many times and been shot at by their soldiers using these more times than I can count."

"Did anybody else use them?"

"They gave about twenty-five thousand to the Americans during the war of independence and exported them all over the place after the Napoleonic war."

"So, this could come from anywhere?"

"Certainly," Marty admitted.

He was handed the uniform coat. It had a bloody hole in the left shoulder.

"I see why someone dropped the rifle."

"Can you tell us anything about it?"

"9th Light Infantry uniform coat. They were disbanded in 1815. Their regimental stores were given to a new regiment called the Legion of Ardennes which was reformed in 1820 as the 1st Light Infantry. See here? The insignia have been removed. Oh," he added as if he had just thought of it, "and the 9th was also reformed in 1820 but with a new uniform."

Ha! The Frenchman is not as clever as he thought. He tells the truth but not all of it, the king thought triumphally.

"How is it that you know so much?"

"Your Majesty, as an officer of his Majesty's Royal Navy, I make it my business to know as much about our former enemy as I can."

"But you are at peace."

"And I thank God we are. War is so tiresome. However, old habits die hard. The peace has not lasted as long as the war."

Escalation

The French Envoy was made a permanent fixture at the court as Ambassador and the king played him off against Marty in a sort of game which both were wise enough to see through. Neither overtly attacked the other, keeping relations cordial. Cyril's wife arrived a month or so after the permanent residence was approved from Saigon.

Caroline took her under her wing, and a friendship of sorts grew. Marty and Cyril also got on well. Their conversation carefully excluded anything to do with foreign policy.

After more staff arrived from Vietnam, the French organised a ball inviting all the diplomats and their senior staff in Ava with their wives/mistresses.

In 1819 Bagyidaw sent an army of some thirty thousand men to Manipur to bring Raja Marjit Singh into line. He had the audacity to not attend the king's coronation as he was obliged and did not even send an embassy with tributes. Then he declared independence.

The deeply offended king, reconquered Manipur, kicked Singh off the throne and attempted to capture him. However, he escaped to his brother's kingdom of Cachar which was a British protectorate. From this protected base the brothers mounted hit and run raids on Burmese forces and establishments across Manipur. The king called for Marty.

"You must stop these pirates from attacking my kingdom."

"I can but try, your Majesty. Cachar is a protectorate not a subsidiary, so my government has limited influence."

"Then withdraw your protection. I will deal with them myself."

"I will travel to Cachar and speak to them. May I have your permission to travel across the country?"

"Go, as soon as possible."

Marty sent a dispatch to Calcutta telling them that he would be visiting Cachar. He didn't elaborate on why; they could figure that out for themselves. He had been receiving a steady stream of intelligence on the border and the goings on of the Singhs so nothing the king had said had surprised him.

Caroline's first priority was the ball and the preparation for that. They received papers and magazines from London which were only a few months old on a pair of diplomatic packets run by the admiralty. This was a unique fast courier service used by the Foreign Office and Secret Service out of Falmouth that delivered mail to Calcutta. Mail for Marty was collected by either the Pride or Unicorn and delivered to the residence.

The packet ships were clippers similar to the Pride and designed for speed. They sacrificed cargo capacity for long thin hulls and an abundance of sail, could average fifteen knots and even peak at twenty. With ample crew they could sustain that speed for twenty-four hours a day doing the run to Calcutta in forty days. Apart from dispatches, important diplomats could be carried in relative comfort.

The net result of all that was a mad dash to get the latest London fashions replicated in local fabrics. She chose a round dress of delicate pale cream net that carried a thin vertical stripe of blue over a white satin slip. It was high waisted in the latest style with a round-cut neckline that just exposed her cleavage, edged with quilling of the finest tulle. She opted for daring off the shoulder half sleeves that were full and puffed. The hem was ankle length and extended by a double rouleau of white satin and an applique of ruffled Crepe-Lisse. Delicate satin slippers and a fascinator finished off the ensemble. Older dresses were sacrificed to scavenge materials that couldn't be obtained locally.

Sebastian would accompany Melissa. Sir Raymond was single and asked the daughter of a British merchant he had made the acquaintance of to accompany him. Peter declined to attend as he said he couldn't dance so Adam took his place.

The evening of the ball they walked to the French residence where a huge pavilion had been erected to cover a dance floor. A band of sorts had been assembled which tooted and scraped popular tunes and a large buffet was available in a smaller pavilion. Prominent members of the expatriate community were also invited, and Marty soon found himself surrounded by people wanting to be seen with the ambassador or who wanted to make his acquaintance.

Caroline was busy with their wives until Marty broke away from the crowd and danced with her.

"Lord, this ambassador thing can be a pain."

"I know, I have had four requests to soirees that are blatant attempts to get you to favour their husbands with the king. Good Lord, who is Adam dancing with?"

Adam was dancing with a very striking Burmese girl, one of only a few present.

"She knows how to dance in European fashion. She is very elegant," Marty noted.

"He looks enchanted."

"I think she is the only person in the room as far as he is concerned."

After the dance Marty found Cyril.

"Who is that girl?"

"The one dancing with your man? Why, that is Princess Mima."

Marty frowned. "What's a princess doing here?"

"I invited the king, who declined. But he said he was having several of his daughters trained in European dance and languages who he would like to attend. She is the daughter of, I think, his fourth wife. The other two are dancing with the sons of my secretary."

Marty had decided they would travel on horseback as that would be faster than trying to take a carriage across Burma. So, two days later he, the Shadows (less Roland who was still recovering from his wound), Chandra and a squad of Burmese cavalry mounted up outside the residence. All the Europeans carried rifles in saddle holsters and revolvers on their person. Marty was relieved that he was taking Adam with him. Since the ball his man was a little distracted and showing signs of, well, being lovestruck. The trip would let him get his mind sorted out.

Marty's horse was skittish and hard mouthed. He had probably been ridden by a poor horseman in the past who had been too hard on the reins. Marty was a good enough horseman to control him without hauling on the reins or resorting to a crop. The officer in charge of the cavalry waited patiently for Marty to give the order to move out.

He got his horse settled and looked up to the balcony around the first floor where Caroline and the wives were assembled to wave them off. He raised his hat and blew her a kiss. She waved a handkerchief in return. They had said their goodbyes the night before.

"Let's go," he cried and kicked his horse forward. The sound of the horse's hooves loud in the dawn light. A train of twelve pack horses brought up the rear led by a pair of Burmese soldiers. It was expected that it would take ten to twelve days to reach Silchar, the capital of Cachar.

The escort would be with them up to the border between Manipur and Cachar and act as guides as well as protection. The officer had told him through Chandra that they would overnight at military outposts and forts where they could, if necessary, obtain replacement mounts.

The first day they covered around forty miles in Marty's estimation. The roads were fair and laid out with the obvious intention of being able to move troops around efficiently. The horses settled down and, when they got to the first stop, their riders gave them a good rubdown and fed them oats and hay, refusing the help of the army grooms.

Matai checked the horses with the help of Sam who wanted to learn about their care, much to Marty's surprise. The two carefully cleaned out stones and packed earth from hooves and applied oil. Any signs of saddle sores were treated with liniment. They were watched by curious soldiers and grooms.

The food supplied by the army was nutritious and filling. Marty took note of how they made simple ingredients and the minimum of meat into tasty, spiced dishes that satisfied even the hungriest.

The third day they entered the hills and by the fourth, the hills had grown into mountains. Marty noted the terrain, the location, size and complement of the forts in a notebook in code.

They entered Manipur on the sixth day. The country had an air of oppression. Military patrols were encountered frequently, and villagers didn't greet them as they passed like they did in Burma.

The Shadows formed up around Marty rather than behind him as they had up to the border. Their escort was more alert. Rifles were carried in hand rather than in their saddle holsters.

"Edgy sort of place," Marty commented to Chandra who rode beside him.

"The people do not like being Burmese subjects."

"I can see that."

Chandra spat on the road.

"They are Indians not Burmese."

"Indeed," Marty sighed as he noted the difference in dress and features of the people who lacked the strong Indo-Chinese cast of the Burmese.

They stayed at a large fort that night within twenty miles of the border. The next morning Antton and Sam rode to the border and informed the guards that the British ambassador to Burma would be arriving at midday.

Marty and the Shadows arrived at the border where there was a tense standoff between their escort and the Cachar border guards. He was told he had to wait. After about thirty minutes a troop of Indian cavalry appeared, and the officer came forward.

"Captain Josyula, 3rd Bengal Cavalry at your service Lord Stockley. I apologise for arriving a little late, one of our horses went lame."

The guards stepped aside, and Marty with his men crossed into Cachar.

"Pleased to meet you, Captain, shall we proceed?"

"Of course."

The Burmese cavalry rode away.

"You keep a permanent presence in the province?" Marty asked as they trotted along.

"Enough to dissuade the Burmese from raiding across the border. They do not want a fight with either Indian or Company forces."

Marty nodded and took in the scenery. This was definitely India, provincial differences notwithstanding. He savoured the smells and sights feeling quite at home.

The capital was not large but neatly laid out around an imposing palace where Raja Singh and his brother resided.

The city was surrounded by a defensive wall, and they entered via a gate. Inside there was a relaxed atmosphere and street vendors called out their wares and the smell of street food permeated the air.

The palace of Chourjit Singh was not large by Indian standards but then neither was his kingdom. They were met by a plethora of servants and their baggage taken inside.

"You will be shown to your rooms where you can recover from your journey and refresh yourselves before meeting the Raja and his brother."

In his luxurious rooms, servant girls prepared a bath and made as if they would stay and wash his back. Adam chased them out.

"I am sure Lady Caroline would not approve," Adam said as Marty lowered himself into the hot water and sighed. He lit a cheroot.

"I'm sure she wouldn't," a familiar voice said.

"Hello, Frances, I wondered if I would find you here." Marty smiled and blew a smoke ring towards the ceiling.

Frances Ridgley, MBE, was the resident intelligence agent for the British in India and a very old friend of Marty. The two men were of an age and their relationship went back to before the Peninsular war.

Frances pulled up a chair and sat so he could see his old friend's face.

"You are looking well."

"So are you. A bit of salt in your hair but you look fit."

"Still smoking those things when Caroline can't stop you, I see."

"I enjoy the odd one. Are you behind the raids?"

"Not directly. The Singhs are bent on revenge for Marjit losing his kingdom. I just feed them information."

"I'm supposed to ask them to stop."

"Wouldn't do any good," Frances said dismissively. "How are Caroline and the children? I hear Beth graduated with flying colours."

"She is in South America dealing with a pirate problem in cooperation with the Americans. James is in the Mediterranean with the Flotilla helping the Greeks gain independence. The twins have been separated at last and are pursuing their own careers. Constant wants to be a horse breeder and doctor and Edwin wants to join the cavalry."

"Perfect. The government wants the Singhs to provoke the Burmese into doing something that will give them an excuse to respond," Frances said.

"And if they don't?"

"Then we will encourage Assam to rebel."

Marty finished his cigar and proceeded to wash himself. Frances waited until Marty stood. He handed him a towel. Adam arrived with a robe.

"You have a few more scars."

"Comes with the territory."

Marty and Frances talked long into the night catching up on all that had happened since they last met. In the morning the two were found sitting at a table with the Singh brothers.

"The king of Burma wants me to ask you to stop raiding his forces in Manipur. Let's just assume I did, and you refused so we can get onto other business," Marty said after Francis had introduced him.

"Nothing has changed, they took my throne illegally," Marjit said bitterly.

"And we will get it back, but for the sake of form we need them to make the first move," Francis said.

"Can you step up your attacks?" Marty asked.

"We only have a few men," Chourgit responded calmly.

"Recruit from the dissatisfied in Manipur. Set up cells of locals to disrupt Burmese traders and merchants. That will stretch their military because they will have to protect them. That in turn will make their military easier targets," Marty said.

"Lord Martin has done this before in other countries. He is an expert in guerrilla warfare and insurrection."

"Can you not stay and teach us?"

"Unfortunately, not, I have to go back to Ava. However, I have a man who works for me who can come here and assist you."

"Sebastian?" Francis grinned.

"None other. He and one other will be mysteriously recalled to England, but their ship will bring them to Chattogram, and they will make their way here."

The brothers grinned happily at this.

"In the meantime, here is a map with all the forts I saw on my way across Manipur."

"The Pride will be waiting for me in the Meghina river. It will take me back to Ava," Marty told Frances over breakfast.

"Won't that annoy the king?"

"I hope so. There is a war party which wants to take much more direct action over Assam and Manipur. My presence gives the king hope he can settle this peacefully. I need to wean him off me bit by bit, so their influence is increased."

"That is a dangerous game, my friend. He or they may just decide to remove you."

"That has always been a risk."

A three-day ride saw them at the river where a boat took them down to the delta where the Pride waited. She sailed at top speed to the Irrawaddy River and up to Thayet where river boats were waiting to take them to Ava.

"Sebastian, you have been recalled," Marty told him when he arrived. "I called in at Calcutta and you have new orders. You will take Antton with you, his son is ill."

Sebastian took the proffered envelope noting that the seal was unusually thick.

"I better get packed then." He shook Marty's hand and as he turned caught sight of one of the Burmese cleaning girls hovering almost out of sight behind a door.

Marty, who deliberately had his back to her, winked. Sebastian nodded and made his way to the other door that led from the room. Marty was satisfied that in an hour the king would know when George told him.

The king was not annoyed that Marty had taken the Pride back to Burma but was suspicious of why he hadn't taken her for the outbound trip. Marty's excuse was he had received orders to speak to the governor of India in Calcutta. When asked, 'what for?' he politely but firmly declined to answer. The king was displeased and dismissed him with an annoyed wave of the hand.

Ambush off the Andermans

Sebastian sat on the deck of the Unicorn under a canvas shade as they sailed down the Irrawaddy. He had the order packet in hand and used a sprung switchblade knife (a recent addition to his armoury) to split the over-thick seal in two. The upper seal of the Foreign Office broke away to reveal Marty's personal seal underneath.

What are you up to, Boss?

He ran the knife under the seal and opened the packet. Inside there were five sheets of blank paper to bulk it out and one in code. He, like Marty, had the code memorised and read it without decrypting it.

Sebastian

I want you to go to Cachar and help the Raja and his brother to create an insurgency in Manipur. I don't need to tell you how to do that, suffice to say that the Manipuri's are ripe for rebellion.

Frances Ridgley is there and will help with intelligence. Listen to what he says and ask questions as he can sometimes assume you know more than you do.

Take your time and make sure the network is secure as the Burmese are good at extracting information, as you know. You may have to sacrifice a cell or two to make sure the Burmese know that the Cacharies are behind them, but you do not want them to be able to clean up your network from that.

You will also need to start supporting a rebellion in Assam but that comes second as I hope the rebellion in Manipur will be enough.

I have given you Antton to help. Please apologise to him for me for misleading him about his son's health.

"Is that from Martin?" Antton said as he walked over.

"It is."

"My boy is fine, isn't he?"

"He is and Martin apologises for misleading you and causing any worry."

"I knew he was lying when he told me in front of that cleaner who spies for the king."

Sebastian chuckled.

"He told me I was recalled in front of her too."

"So, what are we going to be doing?"

"Making trouble for the Burmese in Manipur and Assam."

"Nice." Antton smiled as he looked out over the passing paddy fields. "I like a good rebellion."

The Unicorn left the river delta and set a course west by south. Wolfgang wanted to give the impression they were going to Madras where Sebastian and Antton were supposed to be picking up a Company liner back to England.

"A junk has dropped in behind us," Gordon McGivern reported.

"Let's see how fast she can go. Make all sail," Wolfgang ordered.

The junk was a typical Burmese design. Long with a narrow beam, raised stern castle, sixty oars, main and fore masts with large single square sails. They were designed to intercept ships at speed not for a long stern chase and Wolfgang knew that.

The Unicorn picked up speed as the sails were set and trimmed. Heeling over to show her, not too clean, copper.

She needs her bottom cleaning, Wolfgang thought.

"Twelve knots and a fathom!" the log man shouted from forward.

"That's not very good," Gordon grumbled.

"We will stop over at the Calcutta yard and clean her bottom on the way back," Wolfgang growled.

The junk kept pace with them to start with by using her sails and oars. However, that was not sustainable and after an hour she started to fall behind.

"We will be out of sight in three hours." Gordon calculated by taking four sightings on the junk's receding mast.

Arnold Grey, the master, agreed. "Aye that should see our masts below their horizon."

"Maintain this course for five hours then steer due west into the Bay of Bengal. Call me if anything happens, I will be in my cabin."

"What did he mean by 'if anything happens,'" Arnold asked with a concerned look.

"I think he expects trouble," Gordon replied.

Their course would take them between the Andaman Islands and the southern tip of Burma. An area known for pirates and an excellent place for an ambush.

"I want double lookouts at the mastheads, changed every hour," Gordon ordered.

Arnold Grey walked over to the rail and seemed to sniff the wind. He looked up at the pennant flying from the mainmast. He frowned and scanned the horizon, his hand shading his eyes. Finally, he went to the chart hut and checked the barometer that swung there.

Gordon watched him and frowned. The master was famous for his weather sense.

"What is wrong, Arnold?"

"Winds shifting and dropping."

"It is?" Gordon had not felt anything."

"Aye, and it's going to drop more. Barometer is rising."

He was right, a zone of high pressure was building over the region and killing the wind.

"Deck, sails to the south."

"Mr Hepworth, my compliments to the captain and tell him the wind is dropping and there are sails to the south."

Wolfgang heard the hail and felt a very small change in the way the ship was working, so was not surprised when the midshipman knocked on his door. Dismissing him he pulled on his coat and hat, clipped on his sword, and took a pair of revolver pistols from his sideboard. He placed caps on the nipples and clipped them to his belt under his coat.

"I have the deck," he called as he stepped onto the quarterdeck. "Report."

"Wind is dropping and we see sails to the south and coming up behind us."

"What are they?"

"Junks."

"It's as Martin thought, the king has decided to thin us out."

"Thin us out, Sir?" Fourth Lieutenant Eden said.

"Yes, he wants Lord Martin to be only able to use one ship."

"I don't understand, Sir. I thought we were on good terms with the Burmese."

Wolfgang gave the young lieutenant a long look.

"How long have you been on this ship?"

"Since the beginning of this voyage, Sir,"

"And when you joined the admiral explained our role?"

"He did, Sir."

Wolfgang waited.

"Oh," Eden said, eyes going wide as he finally got the idea.

Wolfgang smiled, "Good you understand, now take the ship to quarters we have some 'pirates' to thin out."

The Unicorn quietly prepared for war. Guns were loaded but not run out. The armourer brought up the sharpening wheel and was busy honing weapons. They had done this many times before and there was a calmness that a stranger would have thought unusual for men about to commit murder on a large scale.

"Bording nets are set, main battery loaded with small ball over canister, carronades with grape and chain." Gordon McGivern reported, "The swivels are loaded with canister, and grenades have been brought up."

"We will let them get close before we give them the benefit," Wolfgang replied. "A cable should do nicely."

A cable or two hundred yards would allow the shot to spread nicely and allow for direct shooting. With all guns firing at once, the Unicorn would be enveloped in a wall of iron. Marty and Wolfgang had come up with this strategy over coffee on the veranda of the residence. With the Unicorn's gun crews ability to reload in well under two minutes. This could be repeated at least once more before any ships or boats could get close enough to board. Then the swivels would be brought into play. Each gun crew was armed with a pair for each mount. As one was fired it would be replaced by the other which was pre-loaded. A third crewman would act as loader.

When the junks were a mile away, they split into two groups of four and two of two. They would use their standard tactic of trying to envelop their prey and board from all sides.

"Clew up the mains."

Sebastian and Antton held rifles at the ready and each had a large bore blunderbuss slung across their backs.

They, along with the marine sharpshooters would pick off steersmen and obvious officers.

The junks were being rowed and speeding towards them. Five hundred yards off they fired their bow chasers. Most missed, but a couple of large stone shot hit the sides. The Unicorn was built of three layers of oak and shrugged off the impacts.

"Ready, men!" Wolfgang roared in a voice that could be heard from bow to stern.

The men rose from where they had been sitting on the deck and manned their guns.

"Run out!"

The deck shook as the big eighteens were run out, the big forward carronades hut collapsed. Gun Captains' arms were raised to indicate their readiness.

Gordon waited for the ship to roll to the level.

"FIRE!"

The noise was incredible as all her guns fired at once making her timbers creak. A wall of iron howled across the water in an ever-expanding cloud of death and destruction.

Small ball smashed timbers and mashed bodies. The cannister swept the decks killing and wounding, The gun crews had not aimed but set their elevation so the shot was centred at a height just above the oar ports of the junks.

The attack faltered as oarsmen were killed and their stroke disrupted, giving the Unicorns' precious extra seconds to reload.

"FIRE!"

Between the broadside the Riflemen were busy. The ones in the tops were shooting down into the junks, Antton and Sebastian fired from the quarterdeck trying to pick off the steersmen of the junks trying to get up behind them. Both had put wax in their ears and bound their heads with bandanas to protect them from the incredible noise.

The smoke from the guns drifted away and a junk emerged. Its bow and rigging severely damaged and only the last two thirds of its oars in use. Sebastian could see the steersman at the big oar at the back. He sighted, compensated for the movement of the ship, and squeezed the trigger. The man fell but the ship came on. He reloaded and fired again, taking out the drummer who coordinated the rowers. Beside him Antton was keeping up a steady rate of fire on the second ship.

The second broadside roared out when the junks were just fifty yards away. Only one had any rigging left, all were damaged. But they came on and got alongside, below the guns.

"Close ports!"

The guns were already run back from the recoil of the broadside and the ports slammed down. Gunners switched to the swivels and fired down into the boats coming alongside. Other men took grenades from the boxes lined up on the centreline and lit them from slow matches burning over buckets of water. They stepped forward and tossed their lethal toys into the junks.

Screams rose up but still the pirates came on.

Sebastian dropped his rifle and switched to the blunderbuss. He stepped up to the side and aimed down into the ship beside them. The gun had a kick like a mule and sent a mixture of musket balls and scrap metal down into the mass of men crowding the rail to climb the side.

A head appeared over the rail, and he used the gun as a club, swinging it like a cricket bat by the barrel. There was a resounding crack as it connected, and the man dropped out of sight. He discarded the gun and pulled his pistol and sword.

The next head that appeared was shot at point blank range. The man behind him must have thought all he would have to face would be a blade. He was wrong, Sebastian pulled the hammer back, cranking the next chamber into line.

Sebastian's adrenalin was pumping at full force, time slowed, he shifted his aim and shot the second man. The bullet entered his skull, flattening and expanding as it went. The shock wave turning the brain to jelly. It exited above his right ear taking a two-inch diameter chunk of skull and his brains with it.

The fight was vicious and uncompromising, the officer's' revolvers making a significant difference. Many pirates were felled before they gained the deck. If they were hit centre-body or head, they mostly died. If they were unlucky and were hit in the arm or leg the damage would still be catastrophic as the limb could be shattered or even shot off.

The marines used bayonets and boarding pikes, the crew cutlasses, pikes, tomahawks, even hammers. The cook was seen with a pair of cleavers laying on with gusto.

Gradually the sound of fighting was replaced by the groans and cries of the wounded. It was over. Sebastian had time to reload his pistol and walked around the deck giving the coup de grace to any wounded pirates. Of the twelve junks that initially attacked them only two made it away. The butcher's bill? Two Unicorns were seriously wounded, five lightly. They counted over forty dead pirates on deck, but God only knew how many died in the ships. Superior weaponry and tactics had won the day.

Manipur

Sebastian and Antton rode through the main gate of Silchar and there to meet them was Frances. They dismounted.

"How did you know we would be here now?" Sebastian asked as they shook hands.

"I had men watching the road. Welcome to Cachar Lancelot," Francis replied using his code name.

"Thank you, R. M sends his regards," Sebastian replied. Frances, like Marty, was senior enough in the service to only have a single letter designation.

That was all the confirmation that was needed. Frances turned to Antton, "Hello, old man."

"See you don't need a cane yet, you old codger," Antton fired back.

They both laughed and embraced.

Frances led them through the town to a large house surrounded by a wall with a guard on the gates. The man snapped to attention and called for the gates to be opened. They walked inside, their train of horses following.

"What did you bring?" Frances asked as servants started to unload the long heavy boxes.

"Muskets, Indian army issue and swords also made in India."

"Excellent." Francis turned to the Indian overseeing the unloading. "Ronit, store the boxes in the stables and have their bags taken to their rooms."

"Yes, Sahib."

"Come, let's get you settled in."

Once settled in they were taken to the palace and introduced to the Singhs.

"What is your experience in this?"

"I have most recently been an advisor to the Armies of Independence in South America, but before that I was with Lord Martin in the Peninsula where we set up and assisted Spanish and Portuguese rebel groups in their fight against the French."

"What do you advise that we do?"

"Recruit locals and organise them into cells of six or seven men, one per village or region. Do not tell them about the other cells, that way if one cell is compromised then the others cannot be," Sebastian explained. "We will arm them and train them. We have brought guns and swords."

The Singhs looked at each other and seemed to come to an unspoken agreement.

"When do we start?"

Sebastian had the Singhs send out men into the Manipur countryside to find recruits. They would visit villages that were known to hate the Burmese oppression and talk to the head man. He would put forward six or seven men, preferably young and single, who they would train. Former soldiers who had been disbanded after the Burmese invasion were particularly sought after.

In the meantime, Sebastian and Antton slipped into Manipur and set up a training camp in the Khoupum Valley which was in the mountains between Loktak Lake and the Cachar border. It was well hidden in the forest but close enough to the trail to the border for supplies and weapons to be brought in by pack horse. Messages were sent out by pigeon. They had brought a cage full, from Burma, that were trained to fly to the residence, but they could only afford to send one a month.

It was not long before small groups started to arrive, brought in by their recruiters. They were instructed that no names or home village locations should be shared and a cadre of 'training assistants' enforced that rigorously. Recruits with military experience were employed to teach the young recruits weapon skills and soon the camp rang to the sound of practice swords smacking against training posts and the bang of muskets.

Sebastian and Antton taught tactics and sabotage skills, how to set up and execute ambushes and some unconventional, fighting skills. The young men were enthusiastic and learnt fast. They even came up with the idea of giving themselves code names all on their own and proudly introduced themselves to their trainers. After that, every man was given a code name as soon as he arrived from a list that one of the sergeants created.

An unexpected bonus was the arrival of a Maratha warrior that Frances had recruited. Ojas Phalkes was a fierce moustachioed fellow who was an expert in guerrilla warfare (Shiva Sutra). The Marathas had been scattered after the Anglo-Maratha war and he had become a mercenary rather than join the colonial Indian army.

His tactics were suited to the mountainous and wooded regions of Manipur and complemented Antton and Sebastian's tactics in open country.

After three months, the first cells were sent back to their villages fully armed and prepared. The Burmese, their officials and collaborators started to suffer. Collaborators and officials were found hanging from trees in the dawn light, their premises burning to the ground. Lone Burmese soldiers were ambushed and killed, their weapons stolen and bodies displayed naked and sometimes mutilated.

In Burma the return of an unscathed Unicorn was not received well in the court. The king threw a tantrum, and the admiral was executed. The loss of ten ships was not acceptable. Marty watched the shenanigans from a safe distance with his agents keeping him informed.

Sebastian had developed a network of agents that reached into the palace itself and Marty had taken it over. Regular reports via dead drops were received and collated, the information used to decide what to do next.

There was a rise in the influence of the war party led by General Maha Bandula and supported by Queen Me Nu and her brother, the Lord of Salin. Marty on the other hand was reduced to one meeting a month.

Reports started to trickle through about a rise in raids and resistance near the Cachar border with Manipur. Local officials appointed by the Burmese were turning up dead and their offices burnt. The temperature rose but annoyingly didn't reach boiling point.

Marty focussed on setting up a way of getting messages quickly to Sebastian. Pigeons were good for getting information from him, but it was taking weeks to get messages back the other way. What he needed was a telegraph chain but there was no way the king would let him do that. In any case, it would provide the Burmese with an easy way to get messages north as well.

Sebastian and Antton left the camp and made their way down out of the hills towards Imphal the capital of Manipur. They were dressed as locals and had dyed their skin using walnut oil. They were accompanied by Ojas Phalkes and one of Frances's agents. Posing as merchants with a train of pack horses they dropped down into the wetlands that formed most of the Imphal valley.

The village of Nambol provided a convenient place to stay and they had the opportunity to re-supply the local cell and pick up the latest intelligence. The capital was crawling with Burmese troops and regular cavalry patrols would go out to patrol the valley and foothills. The gate, however, was relatively unguarded and they could enter without being checked.

The city was busy with shopkeepers hawking their wares and a busy market for vegetables and meat. They made their way to a warehouse on the east side of town and rode into the courtyard. A robed man with an impressive turban came out to meet them.

"I have a consignment of Bombay duck," Sebastian said in Hindi.

"Have the feathers been removed?"

"Only from the gills."

"Come inside."

Large doors were opened, and the horses led inside. Men came and unloaded the paniers which contained genuine trade goods as well as weapons for the revolution.

Sebastian and Antton were taken to an office that was more like a sitting room leaving the other two to look after the goods.

"May Shiva bless you, please sit down, you can call me Bhains," he said in perfect English.

Bhains was Water Buffalo in Hindi which was an appropriate code name for the portly man.

"I am Lancelot," Sebastian replied, "and this is Dagger."

"The governor general is very unhappy with the upsurge in raids."

"Is that what they think? That all the attacks are cross border raids?" Sebastian said.

"Yes, they refuse to believe that lowly peasants could threaten them."

"Interesting, do they think of the Hindus as second-class citizens?"

"Very much so, which plays into our hands as we can start rumours that they will impose Hinduism."

"There is nothing like the fear that your religion will be attacked to stir up the masses, how will you go about it?"

"At the temples, just mention it to the right people and it will spread like wildfire."

"Is there a direct action that can be taken?"

"The best would be for the Burmese to raid a temple but how can we goad them into doing it?"

Sebastian gave it some thought.

"Do they have agents watching the temples?"

"There are agents everywhere."

"I have an idea."

Two days later, after dark, a handcart delivered two long boxes to the temple of Shri Krishna. The boxes were heavy as it took two men to carry them inside. The men were furtive and obviously didn't want to be seen. They left with the empty handcart.

The governor general was informed and asked his advisors what the boxes could possibly contain. When one said they were typical of the type that muskets were carried in he decided that they should be investigated.

A patrol of infantry was dispatched in the morning under the command of a young officer. He marched his men through town to the temple which was located near to a busy market. The men surrounded the small temple, and he pounded on the door demanding entry. The priests waited long enough for the people in the market to notice what was going on then let him in.

The boxes were still lying in the middle of the floor. He looked them over and noticed as they had strange markings in script he couldn't read. He demanded they open the boxes and the priests declined saying they held holy relics. The priests looked afraid, and the young man didn't believe them.

"Why are you afraid? What are you hiding?" he shouted into the older priest's face.

Getting no answer, he ordered two of his soldiers to open them.

The lids were nailed down, and the men resorted to smashing the timbers with their gun butts. The sound drew even more attention outside, and a crowd was gathering.

The officer pulled some of the smashed timbers aside and his eyes widened in horror. Inside was a statue of Kali in black marble, four armed, holding a severed head in one hand, a sword, a trident and a cup in the other three. Her eyes were red, and fangs protruded from her mouth. Her right foot on the chest of Shiva lying serenely before her.

The priests chanted prayers. The crowd started to shout angrily. The soldiers had smashed open the second crate to find a statue of the goddess Parvati but this time a clumsy blow had knocked her nose off. A priest cried out and the word spread like wildfire. The crowd rioted. The soldiers panicked and shots were fired.

"A full scale riot?" Frances exclaimed as Antton recounted what had happened.

"Nothing less," Sebastian confirmed with a grin. "The soldiers panicked and started shooting."

"Anybody killed?" Frances said, looking hopeful.

"They only wounded two people."

Frances looked disappointed.

"But one soldier was beaten to death," Sebastian said.

Frances cheered up.

"They attacked the governor's residence and he had to evacuate his family to the fort. It was burnt to the ground."

Francis was fairly bouncing in his seat with glee.

"Excellent, excellent."

But he was to be disappointed, the Burmese didn't invade or even raid Cachar. They imposed a military curfew, brought in extra troops and the oppression increased. It was time to up the ante.

Assam

Marty was pleased with the reports he got from Sebastian but disappointed the king didn't let the war party off the leash. He needed an extra push. Like Manipur, Assam was ready to rebel and could probably do the trick. All it needed was a spark and some weapons. Well, both could be provided.

He sent a message on the next ship to Calcutta requesting that a large shipment of weapons be sent to Cachar as soon as possible. They would get there in three or four months. Second, he needed Sebastian and Antton to provide the spark, so he sent them coded orders to escalate. Third, a very difficult third, he needed to intercept the reports the king was getting and 'adjust' them'. Which was much easier said than done.

He went into Sir Raymond's office.

"Morning, Ray, do you write Burmese as well as speak it?"

"Good morning, Sir. Yes, I do."

"Excellent. How do you feel about going for a trip up country?"

"Anywhere in particular?"

"I have heard that Monywa is beautiful this time of year."

Marty asked for and got permission to take his family on a sightseeing trip to Monywa. The king even offered him an escort which he politely declined. His monthly meetings had been less cool of late, and detente seemed to be the king's preferred stance. He needed to change that.

They left early in the morning and travelled by carriage and horseback. Monywa was ninety miles a little north of west of Ava and with the dubious roads would take two days to reach if not three. The carriage was an open landau type with old fashioned suspension, so Caroline padded the seats out with cushions to make the ladies more comfortable. Their baggage and supplies were carried in a second carriage rather than an ox cart. As was his habit Marty rode with the Shadows. Adam rode shotgun beside the driver of the ladies' carriage.

They were followed. Their tail was spotted as soon as they crossed the river. It was expected and the men following them were quite inept, so Marty left them alone. Apart from being armed, the party looked and behaved like tourists. They would stop at pagodas or interesting sights and sketch them. Marty was a dab hand with watercolours and could dash off a decent impression quite quickly.

Meals and overnight stops were taken in villages, if possible, but they carried tents if they fancied camping out for a night and Roland could cook as well on a campfire as in his kitchen. Most of the locals they passed were friendly, smiling and waving. Children ran beside the carriage in the villages they passed through. His conscience prickled a little at the thought of the country being plunged into war, but then he thought of the people in Manipur.

The valley that the city sat in was unique in that it was in the rain shadow of the Arakan mountains making the local climate hot and dry. Even in January it was a comfortable sixty-nine Fahrenheit. The city was green, with streets lined with Indian Lilac (neem) trees. These forty- to fifty-foot-high trees had a wide canopy which provided shade and had abundant, fragrant flowers in the summer months.

They had arranged to use the house of a merchant that Marty knew for their stay and were met at the door by a servant. The merchant was out in the countryside procuring spices to send back to England. Once in, Marty called the Shadows together.

"We know they run a weekly messenger service to the northwest. I want to know when the messengers from and to Assam and Manipur arrive and where they overnight. This is a day's ride from the capital for a messenger on a decent horse, so it makes sense that they stop here. Once we have identified them, I want to be able to get my hands on the message so I and Sir Raymond can modify it to suit our needs."

"How long will we stay here?" Matai said.

"I told the king we would be gone for at least a month. I want us to modify at least two outgoing messages, and the ones reporting back if necessary. When we get back, we will make use of the dirt we dug up on that palace clerk to blackmail him into passing the contents of messages to us."

The boys grinned. Sebastian had them watch selected individuals and they had noticed that one in particular regularly visited the house of another official. On closer observation they found that the two men had a clandestine relationship. Their leverage came from the law in Burma which forbade same sex relationships. The Buddhist religion stigmatised homosexuality as being punishment for sins committed in a past life. If exposed the men could face years in prison or even death.

But that was for the future, now Marty wanted to be able to change some messages to make things easier for Sebastian and Antton in Assam and stir things up in Manipur.

They watched the road that the couriers should take and soon spotted one on a lathered horse coming from the north at dusk. He went directly to the local army headquarters where he left his satchel before going to his quarters. Another rider took the satchel onward to Ava the next morning. That answered the question Marty had about whether the satchels were carried by one rider all the way or posted by a chain of riders.

The headquarters was guarded but not excessively. They obviously felt safe this close to the centre of the country. There were two guards on the door twenty-four hours a day in six, four-hour watches. The watch rota started at midnight.

"We will go in at one in the morning, remove the satchel so that Sir Raymond and I can modify the messages and have it ready to be put back by four," Marty said. "Chin will accompany me, the rest of you will provide cover. You know what to do."

The next courier to arrive was going north and they went into action. The sentries changed at midnight, the men sleepy and not that alert. They plodded around their patrol taking minutes longer than the day watches. Those minutes gave Marty and Chin all the time they needed.

"Go," Marty whispered as the sentry turned the corner.

The two of them sprinted across the road from the wall they had been hiding behind. Chin got there first and stood back to the wall with his hand cupped. Marty stepped into the stirrup and Chin boosted him up so he could grab the sill of a window on the raised first floor. He hauled himself up then lowered a short rope which Chin shinned up in short order. They were in.

The satchel should be held in the clerk's office on the same floor and they quietly checked rooms as they passed them. Marty nearly missed it as it was propped against the side of a desk in shadow. He picked it up and checked the flap. It was only held closed by a wooden peg.

The exit was simple. they dropped directly from the window when Adam on a nearby roof gave them the all-clear signal.

They ran to the house and Sir Raymond went through the contents of the bag as Marty carefully opened each scroll.

"This one is to the commanding officer in Manipur. Basically, tells him to imprison and not execute rebels. Looks like the king doesn't want Martyrs."

"Re-draft it so that it reads to publicly execute any leaders of the rebellion they find."

Sir Raymond looked troubled.

"That will be signing men's death warrants."

"Yes, but I have instructed Sebastian to prioritise the rescue of any men sentenced to death."

That was a downright lie, but he needed Sir Raymond to cooperate right then and there.

Sir Raymond set too. Looking slightly happier but troubled all the same.

Marty took the draft and studied the original. Oh, how he wished John was still alive, but he had a very similar paper and ink. His forgery was identical in appearance, and he carefully rolled it, so it was the same as the original. Now all they had to do was get it back into the headquarters building before staff arrived after dawn.

A week later another courier arrived heading north along with one heading south the next day. They had two sleepless nights. But all was going to plan. The commander of the garrison on the border was told to maintain the number of patrols at the current level, not increase them as his general wanted. A report that two prisoners sentenced to death had been freed by partisans was removed.

Sebastian and Antton decided to split up and cover a province each. Antton took Manipur and Sebastian, Assam. The weapons had arrived, and Sebastian was busy smuggling them into Assam helped by the infrequent patrols along the border. Like Manipur, Assam was very hilly with a range of mountains close to the southern border with the rest of India.

Shillong was the capital and sat on the northern edge of the range. Sebastian chose a secluded valley close on the Cachar side of the border. It was time to up the ante and really get under the Burmese skin.

The first man to arrive was a Brahmin Priest. Sebastian was surprised when the man spoke English and blessed the camp. He was followed by a tall Sikh who identified himself as a sergeant of the now disbanded Assam army. He held a true and enduring hatred of the Burmese and was followed by a steady stream of NCO's and the occasional officer.

Marty had ordered that all the commands be done in English. He wanted the Burmese to know the British were behind the rebellion. He trained them in guerrilla tactics and in modern field skirmishing tactics. When the British came to their aid, he wanted them to be able to integrate with the British force.

Having trained the officers and NCO's, he started them training the men. However, this time he didn't use the cell system. The Burmese were savage in their oppression and atrocities were common, one eyewitness wrote:

...in attacking the house of a rich man, they would tie him with ropes and then set fire to his body. Some they flayed alive, others they burnt in oil and others again they drove in crowds to village Naamghars or prayer-houses, which they then set on fire... It was dangerous for a beautiful woman to meet a Burmese man even on the

public road. Brahmans were made to carry loads of beef,
pork and wine. The Gosains were robbed of all their
possessions. Fathers of damsels whom the Burmese took
as wives, rose speedily to affluence and power.

So, rebellion and the complete elimination of the occupying forces was their goal. However, getting the Burmese to invade a protectorate was Sebastian's. He encouraged them to raid into Assam and the Burmese would chase them to the border. By the summer of 1823 the raids were going deeper and causing more deaths of Burmese and their sympathisers than ever before.

Marty was summoned to see the king.

"Trouble?" Sir Raymond asked, as it was not a scheduled audience.

"I hope so. Have the residence prepare to leave in a hurry." In fact, the residence had been quietly prepared to leave for some time so all that was needed was the final packing.

He exited the grounds to find a troop of infantry waiting for him. They formed up around him and he was marched to the palace. The Shadows followed at a discrete distance.

On entering the palace, the first thing he saw was a head mounted on a pole above the gate. It was the official who they had been blackmailing. He was ushered under guard to the throne room, not the audience chamber.

The king sat on his throne eight feet above floor level and the room was lined with soldiers. George stood before the throne dressed in ceremonial robes.

This should be good, Marty thought and bowed to the king.

"The British are giving sanctuary to rebels and criminals in Assam and Manipur. They are training them in Cachar and Jaintia."

That was the first time Marty had heard Jaintia mentioned.

"You are to leave immediately or face execution."

"Your Majesty…" Marty said but got no further as he was taken a hold of by a pair of soldiers.

The king stood and threw the sword Marty had given him down so it stuck point first into the floor at Marty's feet.

"Go and tell your king that there is no more peace between our countries."

Marty shrugged off the soldiers and took up the sword. He bowed to the king, did a smart about face, and made his exit as dignified as he could.

The king spoke to his generals over a map and ordered them to take Shalpuri Island close to Chattogram. It was the beginning.

Escape

As soon as Marty came through the gate the Shadows surrounded him. They were all heavily armed. At the residence the full marine contingent were stationed at the gate. It was now an armed camp.

Sir Raymond had mobilised the servants and ox carts were already being loaded.

"I thought I said to get ready, not pack," Marty said.

"The boys sent word that our spy's head was decorating the palace gate and I had to assume he talked. All the local servants disappeared as well."

"Well, we have been told to get out of the country immediately, so you did the right thing."

"The king returned the sword?"

"Yes, less the biggest jewels."

Caroline was in the house supervising the packing and loading of their belongings.

"Is it war?"

"It soon will be, I think. I need to send a message to Sebastian, but nothing will get out now except the pigeons to Calcutta that came in a month ago."

Marty quickly wrote an encoded report on a flimsy piece of paper used for pigeon post then copied it five times. The five flimsies were rolled tightly and placed in little leather tubes that were sealed and tied to the legs of five pigeons. All five were let go at once.

He changed from his formal uniform into his fighting uniform, he donned his weapons harness and loaded his rifle and a bell mouth blunderbuss. His pistols were already capped and slid into their shoulder holsters. The blunderbuss was slung across his back, and he carried his rifle. The ensemble was completed by the secretion of a number of knives around his person.

By the time he got outside the household was almost ready to move.

"Where's the bed?"

"We are leaving anything not easily carried behind," Caroline said.

Roland came out of the front door festooned in pots which he dumped in a cart with a clamorous rattle. He rushed back inside and emerged a few moments later came back with a large cloth bundle in his arms.

"My knives!" he explained as he gently placed them on the cart and climbed up.

"Are we ready?" Marty asked.

"As we ever will be," Sir Raymond said.

Marty stepped into the house and entered his office. He went to a box in the corner and opened it. Inside was a large, sealed demijohn of clear liquid which he lifted out. He reached back into the box and removed a waxed paper parcel which had a timer set into the middle. *Fifteen minutes should do it, he thought* and set the timer. He placed the package back in the box and gently put the demijohn back in place.

The carts, led by a carriage with the ladies aboard and escorted by marines, the Shadows, Sir Raymond, Peter De'ath, and Marty, made their way the short drive to the dock where their boats were waiting. There was not a single local in sight. Chandra was already aboard and looked very frightened.

"They killed all of our agents."

"You are the only one?"

"Yes." Chandra looked back to where the residence was located. "Is that smoke?"

Marty checked his watch. It was twenty minutes since he set the timer. "Yes, I set a charge with a couple of gallons of naphtha mixed with palm oil on top. Seems to have done the trick."

Everyone set to getting the baggage on board and they were almost done when Chin galloped up.

"The army is coming, they're upset about the fire. Several got hurt."

Marty grinned, he had expected the Burmese to raid the residence as soon as they left.

"Just throw those last bags on and get us moving!"

The trip down river was nerve-racking. The Burmese oarsmen had been replaced by sailors from the ships over the last few months and they and the marines would take it in turns to speed them along as the wind was in entirely the wrong direction for the square sails.

As they got to the middle of the stream a troop of soldiers arrived at the dock. Muskets were fired but the shots landed harmlessly in the water. Marty forbade the men to return fire. Instead, they concentrated on getting downstream as fast as they could as they had two hundred and forty miles to cover before they reached the relative safety of the ships.

They were pursued by boats carrying soldiers which to start with kept pace with them. However, the soldiers wouldn't row, and the crews got tired quickly because of the pace. Whereas Marty rotated his men every hour and could maintain a much higher average speed.

"We will be at the ships in two days at this rate," he said.

"Will we stop at night?" Caroline asked.

"No, we will keep two oarsmen rowing to maintain steerage."

That was necessary as cavalry were patrolling the banks making it clear that if they set foot on land they would be killed.

The sun set and the rowers gratefully pulled in their oars for the night. All except the foremost pair which was manned and kept up a slow rhythm to keep enough way on for the steering oars to bite. No lamps were lit and they ate a cold supper. Marty only catnapped and was at the tiller for most of the night.

False dawn lit the eastern sky. Marty roused the men and got them back on the oars. The birds sang and the sun peeked its face over the horizon directly to Marty's right. They were on the southbound leg of the journey and could raise a sail, even if it was canted around as far as it would go.

The men had an easier time now and didn't have to row so hard. The shore seemed to rush by, and Marty put a man in the bow with a gun to scare other boats out of their way. Marty had a chart and as they passed a distinctive village, he checked it.

"We've made better time than I expected. That was Thazi, I noticed it's funny-shaped pagoda on the way up. We should see the ships soon," he said around mid-afternoon.

The Unicorn and Pride were anchored in mid-stream after an official arrived, all hot and sweaty, and told them their docking privileges were revoked. He tried to tell them to leave but Wolfgang ignored him. He wasn't going anywhere without Marty, Caroline, and the rest.

It was just after six bells in the afternoon watch when the mainmast lookout shouted down,

"Deck there! Two boats flying the jack approaching."

There could only be one reason both boats were on the river together.

"Mr McGivern please organise crews to bring aboard the baggage of the admiral and his people. Rig a chair for the ladies. Mr Hepworth signal 'boats to the Unicorn' please."

Marty saw the signal and realised Wolfgang wanted them all on the Unicorn. That was safer as the Unicorn was better protected than the Pride and they could sort out the household between the two ships once they were at sea.

"Men get ready to pull alongside the Unicorn he shouted and signalled the second boat to do likewise." Even as they approached, they could see cargo nets being prepared on both sides. Marty signalled the second boat to go down the port side.

As soon as they were tied on, sailors swarmed over the sides and helped the people that needed it to board. A bosun's chair took the ladies up. Cargo nets were lowered from the yards to get the baggage aboard. In all it took thirty-five minutes to get everything aboard. It would take longer to sort it all out. The boats were towed behind. "You never know they might come in handy," Marty said.

"Set the jibs, staysails and spanker. Prepare to weigh anchor!" McGivern bellowed.

Marty looked across at the Pride. She already had her anchor up and down ready to break free.

"Anchor away!"

They started to move. It wasn't a moment too soon as boats were coming out from the harbour full of soldiers.

"Take us to stations, Wolfgang," Marty said and waited until the carronades were manned before walking over to the port aft gun.

"Load with ball please," he quietly asked the gunners.

A cartridge wad and ball were swiftly loaded.

"May I?" Marty said and stepped forward to look along the barrel. He swung the gun around until it pointed between two of the boats coming towards them. He wound the screw to depress the gun just enough. Finally, he cocked the hammer and took up the lanyard. Stepping back, he gave it a sharp tug. The ball landed between two boats and sent up a tremendous fountain of water, soaking the occupants and disrupting their rowing rhythm.

The soaking and the sight of the ship's main armament being run out dissuaded the soldiers from pressing their pursuit. Marty relaxed as they picked up speed. A commotion forward attracted his attention.

Adam was nose to nose with Sir Raymond and the two were shouting at each other.

"THAT IS ENOUGH!" Marty bellowed in a voice that could be heard on the Pride, a cable behind them.

The two stopped shouting and Marty pushed between them.

"What is this about?"

"The fool has brought her with him," Sir Raymond spluttered. Adam was about to angrily respond but Marty just looked at him and said, "Don't."

Adam closed his mouth.

"Who have you brought with you?" Marty asked quietly, a nagging suspicion in his mind.

"Mima," Adam said.

" Princess Mima?"

"Yes."

Sir Raymond looked on expecting Marty to explode in anger and was astonished when he burst out laughing.

"Oh, that will put the cap on it," he laughed, "the king will be incandescent."

It also explained why the army was chasing them.

"Where is she?"

"Caroline took her below."

Marty turned to Sir Raymond, "You were right to be angry. In normal circumstances this would be disastrous, but right now it plays into our hands. The king is likely to do the stupid thing we want him to."

Caroline was in their cabin with Mima when Marty entered. The girl was sat on their bed and had been crying but was still beautiful despite the puffy eyes.

"Martin, you"…"

Marty held up his hand, stepped up to Mima, bent and cupped his hand under her chin to raise her head. He looked her in the eyes.

"Do you love him?"

"With all my heart."

"What were your plans?"

"He said we could get married."

Marty stood and smiled. "Well, we can certainly sort that out once we are in international waters."

"Really?"

"Really."

The smile she gave him was as dazzling as the hug was tight. Caroline smiled and started planning.

The ships made good time, the triangular sails they had set gave them an advantage over the river craft and they had charted the river very thoroughly during their time there. Wolfgang knew the river well enough to maintain headway at night although under reduced sail. Cavalry paced them and they had double lookouts set at night against any attempt at a surprise attack.

Apart from a rather poor attempt to blockade the river with boats tied across the narrows, which they blew to pieces with the forward carronades, they were left alone. That made Marty and Wolfgang highly suspicious and as they worked their way through the delta the ships were on high alert.

Their course took them down the river to emerge into the Andaman Sea southwest of Yangon and there was a reception committee waiting for them.

"Ships ahead, blockading the river," the lookout cried.

Marty wanted a first-hand look at that and scaled the mainmast to the topsail yard. He swept the scene with his telescope some ten miles ahead. "Large junks, probably armed with twelve pounders," he muttered. "Looks like they have moored them at either end of the line and strung them together."

He descended to the deck via a stay.

"Fire ships," Wolfgang said after Marty described what he had seen.

"Easiest way to break their line," Marty agreed.

"Get those boats around to the side and load them with powder casks and combustibles," Wolfgang ordered.

Gordon McGivern, who had heard what Marty had said came forward. "I shall ask for volunteers to man them, and would it be a good idea to rig grapnels in the rigging?"

"Make it so," Wolfgang replied.

All the midshipmen wanted to command the boats and Gordon selected Stirling and Hepworth. There was no shortage of volunteers either and good swimmers were chosen in case the ship's boats they should use to escape were damaged.

Three miles from the mouth of the river the river boats took the lead. Quinten Stirling commanded the first and Robin Hepworth the second. Each river boat towed a ship's boat. A mile from the blockade the Unicorn hove to under backed foresails. The Pride fifty yards off her starboard beam. Both ships were at quarters with their guns run out.

The fire boats continued steadily onwards and raised triangular sails. That was Quinten's idea and they had used a spare pair of the Unicorn's smaller jib sails. It meant they didn't need to row and only needed a skeleton crew in each boat.

To start with the Burmese looked on curiously and waited to see what the English ships would do. They took no notice of the river boats until someone realised that the sails were strange. Even then they did nothing other than watch them. It wasn't until they were a cable away and smoke started coming from them, they got worried.

Quinten got the men into the gig, pulled up at their stern and tossed the lit lantern onto the pile of old sailcloth and other combustibles that had been doused in lamp oil. It smashed with a satisfying whump as the flame ignited the oil. He checked that the boat was heading between the centre two junks and the bindings that kept the rudder oar in the right place were tight.

He looked across at Robin, whose boat was targeting the next join in the chain of junks.

A cannon fired. It was time to go, and he jumped over the stern into the gig. "Get us out of here," he said, and the oarsmen put their backs into it.

He was standing at the stern hand on the rudder when something tugged at his shoulder. His hand fell away from the shaft, and he looked down to see a hole in his uniform with blood seeping out. "Well, I'm damned," he said and dropped to a seat.

"You alright, Sir?" Gav Granger the starboard oar asked him.

"Keep rowing, that lot will go up soon," Quinten said and shifted his position so he could steer with his other hand.

The Burmese sailors tried to fend off the burning boats with oars, but they still wedged themselves in between the tied-up ships and by now were burning furiously. The captains ordered the cables cut that tied the ships together. They were too late; the fire reached the powder.

Marty watched the scene unfold before him. It was a perfectly executed fire ship attack. The mids would be commended for their bravery and the crews rewarded. A resounding explosion ripped the line of junks apart, seriously damaging the junks either side of where the boat had lodged itself and starting fires. A moment later the second boat went up.

"I think we can make way, Wolfgang," Marty said.

"Get those men aboard and get us underway. Make all normal sail. Guns give them a broadside as we pass through."

The Pride dropped in behind and followed them forward. Marty watched the crews come aboard and stepped forward when he saw Quinten being helped.

"He be wounded, Sir. Shot through the shoulder. Gav Granger said as he held the young man up."

"Get him to Mr Shelby, I will be down to see him once we are clear of these junks."

He put his hand on Quinten's good shoulder. "You have done very well, son."

Quinten smiled wanly and said, "Thank you, Sir, it was fun."

Marty got back to the quarterdeck in time to see the guns deal broadsides to the junks either side of the gap they had created. As the smoke cleared the masts blossomed with sail and the frigate sped away from the carnage they had caused. The Pride added to it with her own rolling broadsides leaving burning and sinking junks in their wake.

Calcutta

Adam and Mima were married by Wolfgang two days later after they had cleared the Andaman Islands and were in the Bay of Bengal. Tabetha, who was a better than fair seamstress, made her a wedding dress that was true to her heritage. She looked wonderful and Caroline was her maid of honour. Adam was dressed in his best suit and Marty was his best man.

Wolfgang carried out the ceremony with dignity and it was witnessed by the entire crew. A bullock was killed and the whole ship celebrated.

Marty and Caroline presented the couple with a scroll, "This is for the two of you," Caroline said.

Adam unrolled it and his mouth fell open. The scroll was the title to a cottage on the Cheshire estate.

"My Lord… what can I say?" he stammered.

"You will need somewhere to raise your children. The house is not far from the main house so you can live there and still fulfil your duties."

"And when you travel with Martin, Mima will have the support of the other wives and me."

"And me!" Melissa piped up. She and Mima were becoming firm friends.

A day out from Calcutta they were approached by an East India Company Marine sloop. It was the end of September and the sloop pulled alongside after signalling that he had messages. The lieutenant in command of it came aboard and saluted Marty.

"Lieutenant Rochester, the Sloop Abigail. I was bringing you an urgent dispatch. It was lucky we spotted you."

Marty took it and opened it. He looked grim as he read it.

"Gentlemen, the Burmese have invaded and taken Shalpuri Island. This was our recall," he said to Sir Raymond and Peter De'ath who were stood beside him. "This is the mistake we have been trying to cause and will surely be followed by others."

Marty shook Rochester's hand. "We were kicked out by the Burmese. Now we know why. Thank you. We will continue to Calcutta."

The Abigail stayed with them to Calcutta and Marty reported to the governor general immediately they arrived.

William Pitt Amherst, 1st Earl Amherst was three years younger than Marty and had been appointed in place of Lord Hastings. Hastings had refused to reduce the field pay of the officers of the Bengal army to peacetime levels. Which he got away with while they were at war with Nepal and the Maratha Confederacy but when peace reigned London had enough and removed him from the seat. Now they expected Amherst to do it for them.

Marty was shown straight in. Amherst was not a tall man or overly imposing. He had the look of a man who was frantically treading water in a sea where he was just out of his depth. Which he was. This was his first position as a governor and his inexperience showed.

"Admiral Lord Stockley, welcome to Calcutta. I am pleased you made it safely here."

"Milord Amherst. Thank you, believe me, we are pleased to be here as well."

"Was it a difficult journey?"

Marty took a seat and Amherst sat as well.

"Tea?" Amherst asked.

Marty recounted the goings on in Ava, Amhurst listened intently.

"Then you feel you have accomplished everything you set out to?"

"There is still work to be done by my team in Cachar, but I think the excuse the government wanted, the casus belli, has been delivered in the invasion of the East India Company's Shalpuri Island. However, we can give them an even stronger cause if we can get the Burmese to invade Cachar."

There was a knock at the door and an aid stuck his head through. "Sir Edward, wants to see you."

"He doesn't have an appointment," Amherst said.

"He insists."

Amherst looked unsure again.

"Can I give you a word of advice from someone who has experience of this?" Marty said softly, leaning forward so only Amherst could hear.

Amhurst nodded.

"Send him away and tell him to make an appointment. If you let him just barge in when he feels like it, you will lose control."

A voice from outside roared, "Well, man is he going to see me or not?"

Marty nodded to Amherst reassuringly.

"Tell the general to make an appointment for tomorrow. I am engaged at the moment."

"Oh, for God's sake," came from outside before the aid could react and the door burst open. Marty stayed sitting down. Amherst was about to rise and stopped when he saw that Marty didn't.

Marty looked at Amhurst with raised eyebrows.

"General, as you can see, I am engaged at the moment. If this is not a matter of extreme urgency, then I would ask you to make an appointment for tomorrow," Amhurst said with a hint of annoyance.

"Who the devil?" Paget blurted and Marty looked around. "Stockley?"

"Edward, how are you? Haven't seen you since Portugal," Marty said.

"Lord Stockley is debriefing me on Burma."

"I am and I am afraid there are some things that are not for your ears, old chap. Spy stuff. If I told you I would have to kill you and all that malarkey. I will visit you and brief you on the military stuff later if that's alright with you."

Paget huffed, but he knew who and what Marty was and decided that discretion was the better part of valour and bowed his way out.

"You know him then?"

"He was a major under Wellington in Portugal and I was Arthur's Chief of Intelligence."

"Oh."

"Now I believe that only the Intelligence Service and you need to know who we are and what we will do in Cachar. Generals have a prickly sense of honour when it comes to the clandestine world and can get all huffy about some of the things we do."

Amherst laughed at that.

"Frances told me as much before he left for there. He said you were old friends."

Yes, we go back a long way."

Amherst sat in thought for a moment then asked, "What will you tell Paget? He is Commander in Chief, you know."

"I do, I have information on the Burmese army and their fortifications which he will find invaluable."

Marty turned up at Paget's headquarters without an appointment. Partly because he could and partly because he wanted Paget to have a taste of his own medicine,

"Just tell the general that Admiral Stockley is here to see him," He told the adjutant who was Paget's gatekeeper.

"But you don't…"

"MOVE!"

Marty looked smug as the adjutant snapped to attention then went to knock on the general's door.

"I heard him," Marty heard the cultured tones of Paget's voice. "Show him in."

"Please, Admiral, the general will see you now."

Marty's smile was wicked as he went through the door.

"Hello, Lord Stockley. To what do I owe the pleasure of your company?"

"Good morning, Edward. Lovely day isn't it." He turned to the adjutant, "A fresh pot of tea if you please and shut the door on your way out."

Paget scowled and sat back in his chair. Marty pulled one up at the end of his desk and sat. He pulled a sheaf of papers from the satchel he carried and started to sort through them.

"My Lord?" Paget grumbled.

"Just a moment, aah here we are. This is a list of the Burmese army regiments, their strengths and dispositions as of a month ago." He handed over a sheaf tied together with a treasury tag. He allowed Paget a minute or two to scan the list.

"Elephants?"

"Yes, they use them to break the line."

"How do you stop them?"

"Apparently, apart from shooting it in the head, the elephant is prone to panic when confronted with artillery. At which point it can cause more damage to its own side than the enemy."

Paget put the papers down and looked at Marty expectantly. Marty grinned and passed over a folded map.

"All the fortifications we have been able to identify. Wellington thought you might find them useful. Here is another of the river with depths marked."

"Wellington? He knows you are out here?"

"He chose my military attaché. Oh, here is a detailed list of the Burmese officials and commanders in Manipur and Assam, and finally everything we know about the senior officers you are likely to face."

Paget took the papers and placed them on his desk with his hands on top.

"Who do you work for? And do not say the admiralty because I know better."

"The prime minister personally signed my letter of introduction to the king of Burma and George Canning briefed me. The mission is supported by the Intelligence Service and The Duke of Wellington. If you want specifics, I am an admiral in the navy and a senior member of the Intelligence Service. However, tell anybody I am other than an admiral and an ambassador and whoever you tell will disappear."

"Would I disappear too?"

"Probably not, you are too valuable to the East India Company, but you would certainly gain a new adjutant."

There was a knock at the door and the adjutant entered with the tea. Marty poured them both a cup. When the adjutant left, Paget said, "One of your people no doubt."

Marty just smiled.

"Well, I saw you work with Wellington. I would welcome your help here."

"You are already getting it. We will help get you started, after that it's up to you and the army." Marty finished his cup and stood, "Now I must go, I need to find a house for my people."

"Ask Amherst he's good at organising things like that," Paget said a little scornfully.

"Give him time, he is new at the job. I'm sure he will get his feet properly under the table in time."

Paget snorted a laugh.

"With your guidance he stands a chance."

Amherst did indeed help find a house quickly. He knew an agent and introduced Marty that afternoon. Marty took Caroline with him to see the two properties on offer. Both were charming and they chose the most secluded one that had more rooms. It was vacant, furnished and had minimal staff, so they moved in that afternoon.

Marty immediately started planning for a trip to Cachar. Horses and supplies would need to be obtained in Chittagong and for that he needed gold and silver. That was easy. He went to Frances' office and spoke to the agent watching the shop while Frances was away.

"I am M," he said by way of announcing himself.

"Tinker, Sir. The Isle of Skye is beautiful this time of year."

"Yes, but the storms come in from the west."

"Lord Martin, Frances said you would probably call in."

"Very astute of him, he knows me too well. I need funds to visit him in Cachar."

"Ship passage to Narayanganj, horses and supplies," Tinker said.

Marty chuckled. "You have done this before. I don't need a passage, just the horses and supplies."

"Of course, you have your own ships. I saw them in the harbour."

"What news from Cachar?"

"The Burmese are carrying out atrocities and there is a steady stream of refugees into our territory. Both Lancelot and, aah, Dagger?"

Marty nodded.

"They are coordinating raids into the occupied territories with great success. Assam is primed to revolt," Tinker concluded.

"Where will I find them?"

Tinker went to a large map on the wall with flags pinned on it. There were three gold ones.

"The gold flags are our men. The red strikes that have already been carried out and the blue potential targets for the future. It's updated monthly as we get reports via pigeon. Oh, that reminds me, if you are going to visit, can you take some crates of pigeons with you?"

Marty was busy noting the locations by grid reference and nodded. "Yes, we can."

"How many men will you be taking?"

"Me plus seven."

"The infamous Shadows I suppose."

"Them and a few choice marines."

"I will message our man, Percival in Narayanganj to have the horses and supplies ready for you and a guide. Is there anything else you need?"

"We will be carrying several casks of gunpowder, a two-wheeled cart to carry it would be useful."

"That will be waiting for you. When will you leave?"

"Tomorrow, my wife is making house and it's a good time to be away."

Marty asked for an update on the local situation and received a comprehensive briefing.

Back at the house he prepared. Roland would stay at the house, so he needed an explosives and demolition expert. He went to the building the marines had taken over.

"Marines Richard, Smythe and Filbert, prepare for an expedition. Uniforms as well as civilian clothes."

Richard and Smythe were engineers and Filbert, a scout. They would complement the Shadows nicely.

They boarded the Pride and set sail, it was around four hundred and forty miles to Narayanganj, so they settled down for the thirty-six-hour trip.

Weapons maintenance came first. Guns disassembled, thoroughly cleaned and oiled so that not a spot of rust was present. Swords and knives sharpened to razor edges. Blackjack leather oiled, as were belts and sheaths. Clockwork detonators tested.

"Expecting trouble?" Dunbar said, casting an eye over the weapons. It was unusual to see such care taken.

"Expecting to cause some," Matai said as he polished a set of very nasty-looking brass knuckles with a knife attached. All the men including Marty carried at least one set. They were not interested in fighting fair, only winning quickly.

Marty asked Chin to fence, and the lithe Chinese warrior unfolded from sitting cross-legged on the deck to standing in a single movement, butterfly swords in hand.

The two faced off. Dunbar expected them to launch into a flurry of thrusts and parries but instead they fought in slow motion.

"Why are they doing that?"

"It sets the moves into your muscles," Matai explained. "That way when you fight you don't have to think you just react. Watch, Chin will make a feint with one sword while cutting low with the other. Marty will parry the feint with his knife and bind Chin's other sword with his hanger."

The fight unfolded as Matai said but after Marty bound Chin's blade he advanced, and head butted which caught Chin by surprise and the fight was over.

"You lot do not fight fair. I will have to remember that." Dunbar laughed.

Narayanganj and Cachar

The Pride moored at a dock on the Dhaleshwari river just above where it was joined by the Shitalakahya river, and the local agent joined them. He was Anglo Indian, sweaty and had a harassed look about him. Marty went through the forms to confirm he was who he said he was.

"We need to sail up to the Mitford Ghat, that is where the horses and supplies are."

"Ghat?" Dunbar said.

"Dock, it is Hindi for dock," Percival replied.

"Do we need a pilot?" Marty asked.

"He should be here by now."

They went to the side to see if the missing pilot had arrived and saw in the distance a man bustling towards them. Percival shaded his eyes with his hand. "That's him."

Marty watched him approach on bandy legs. He was wearing trousers under a long coat and a turban on his head. He reached the gangplank and looked up.

"Permission to come aboard, Sahib."

"Granted." Dunbar.

"I am very sorry for being late."

Dunbar took his arm. "It is of no consequence, now we need to go to Mitford Ghat."

It turned out that the dock was just fourteen miles upstream, but it took three hours to get there as the river was incredibly busy and full of undisciplined craft going in every which way. The crew was frazzled by the time they docked having had to fend off innumerable boats and deal with angry boatmen. Percival had taken a hand after the fourth or fifth incident when a crew man asked Dunbar if he could just shoot the next one.

Mitford Ghat was not much of a landing spot, and they had to boat the stores and baggage over to the shore. The horses and a horse-drawn two-wheeled cart were waiting for them along with four heavily armed men. Percival introduced Marty to them.

"This is Partho, he will be your guide. His men will look after the pack horses and carts."

Marty nodded and took in the well-maintained condition of their weapons. These were professionals. Partho returned the compliment.

"Nice guns," he said with an Irish accent.

Marty looked at him in surprise and got a grin that exposed white teeth with a gold crown on the left incisor.

"Me mother is Irish, me father a Sikh. Me real name is Patrick but I go by Partho as it's easier for the boys."

"Ex-army?"

"4th Bengal. Now I work for Percy."

Marty had noticed that 'Percy's' hassled demeanour had vanished and that he was now calm and confident. He concluded that the former was an act.

"Is that gunpowder in those casks?" Partho asked as the men carried them to the cart.

"Yes, and pigeons in the crates," Marty said.

"Frances will be happy to see them. Does he know you are coming?"

Percy interrupted, "I sent him a pigeon yesterday."

"Good, shall we get goin'. I want to be out in the country by nightfall," Partho said.

They mounted up. The saddles didn't have rifle holsters, so they rode with them in hand which made them look a very warlike band. People got out of their way because of it and they moved through the more run-down quarter of the city on a track of road that headed just a little north of east. They came to the River Shitalakahya and crossed by means of what looked like a ramshackle pull ferry that crossed at a narrow point.

"Will that take the weight of the cart?" Marty asked, looking at the barge sceptically.

"To be sure, we built it ourselves as we got tired of getting wet fording the damn stream. We just made it look shitty."

Partho was right, the barge didn't shake or wobble as the heavily loaded cart came aboard and was efficiently pulled across. They reached the village of Tarbo as it was getting dark, they set up camp a little outside.

"Something wrong with that village?" Marty asked.

"Nope, apart from them being a bunch of thieves. They want an extortionate amount just for water. So, fuck them, we camp here."

They all slept well on their bedrolls, and broke camp at first light. Just beyond the village they turned to the northeast. The terrain was a flat, river floodplain. Rice fields predominated as they followed the River Meghna. The land rose steadily in the afternoon after they crossed that river, and they reached the bank of the River Manu by evening.

On the north bank they came across a refugee camp. Marty had Partho question them.

"They came here because they know there is food, and they are far enough from Assam to feel safe. The locals are happy enough to feed them."

"What did they say about conditions at home?"

"Torture, rape, slavery. It's not good there."

After that they moved into the hills, and the going got harder for the horses to the point they doubled up the horses towing the cart. They were close to the border with Assam now.

"Boss, on the hill to the north," Sam said.

Marty looked and spotted a rider sitting on the peak watching them.

"That is a Burmese cavalry soldier," Marty said after he took a look with his pocket telescope.

"Hmm that's bold, they haven't been this far inside Bengal before," Partho said.

Marty signed to Filbert who kicked his horse ahead of them. Partho nodded in approval as his trouble bump was itching as well. They continued on and the man on the hill just watched.

Filbert came back on foot and waited in a spot where the man on the hill couldn't see them.

"Your man up there flashed a signal to someone ahead, I must have been in line to see it. I left the horse in a gully and went forward by foot. They are setting up an ambush around the next blind bend in the trail where the road passes through a wooded section. There be four men either side from what I saw."

"I know that place it's perfect for an ambush," Partho said.

"Matai, take three men and get behind the ones on the left side of the track, you know what to do. Partho you and your men continue on. Filbert, Richard and Adam, you are with me. They dismounted and handed their reins to those that were left.

"When you get to the corner, stop as soon as you get around it as if you have seen something wrong. We will join you later," Marty said.

Marty and his men circled through the woods silently. Marty signalled them to halt as he caught the smell of horses on the breeze. He put on a set of knuckle dusters and pulled his knife from its sheath in the small of his back. The others mimicked him.

The horses were tied to a tree. Marty gave them a wide berth then they spread out with Marty on the right and the others in line to his left. They moved forward and he heard someone mutter something in Burmese. He assumed it was, "Why have they stopped?"

He moved forward in a crouch until he spotted the soldiers and slipped up to a couple of yards behind the one to the right of the line. A glance told him the others were in position. The soldier in front of him raised his musket to aim. Marty moved fast, punched him in the side of the head with the brass knuckles then laid his knife across the neck of the prone body. The man was lucky he was unconscious, so he didn't slit his throat.

Grunts from his left and a squeak let him know the others had moved as fast. He secured his prisoner by tying his arms behind his back and checked the others.

Adam, the next in line, was tying his man. Richard was cleaning his knife. He looked at Marty apologetically. Marty grinned and slapped him on the shoulder, he only needed one or two prisoners and his looked like he was an officer. Filbert's had been hit so hard he had stove the side of the man's head in. He was still breathing so Marty put him down with a swift stab to the artery in the neck.

Partho kicked his horse forward as Marty came out of the woods followed by his men and a couple of prisoners. Matai and his men emerged empty handed.

"You want me to go after the one on the hill?" Chin said.

Marty took a moment to think. "No, let him report back."

Partho had dismounted and was tying ropes around the prisoners' necks. He tossed the ends to the men leading the packhorses. Filbert retrieved his horse and when they were all together, they moved on down the road.

Marty was pleased that the lookout was still in position when they moved into open ground again. He looked up at him and waved.

They crossed the border into Cachar later that day and headed to the capital. It looked to be on a war footing with mounted patrols heading out from the gates. Partho took them straight to the house where Frances was staying.

"Hello, Martin, thought you might turn up," Frances said as he shook Marty's hand.

"Hello, Frances. You know me; can't stay away from a good fight."

The two laughed and embraced.

"Come in and sit. I see you brought the boys with you."

"I intend to push things to the brink. General Paget is fired up and ready to move."

Matai and Chin entered with the prisoners who were staggering from the extended walk they had been forced to endure.

"Present for you. These are two of only three survivors of an attempted ambush." Marty smiled.

"What happened to the other one?" Frances said as he poured water into a teapot from his large steaming samovar.

"Let him go and report to his seniors."

"Put them over there in the stress position," Frances said, nodding to a bare wooden area of floor. He rang a bell and a servant girl came in.

"Be a darling and ask Padu to come in." She bobbed a curtsy and left without saying a word.

"We have three crates of pigeons for you as well," Matai said.

"Thank the Lord for small mercies! I am down to my last pair. Would you be so kind as to put them in the pigeon loft at the back of the house?" Matai left, leaving Chin to watch over the prisoners.

"What are Sebastian and Antton up to?" Marty asked.

"Annoying the Burmese by assassinating their collaborators and officials, stealing their goods and burning the odd property. They are doing a good job."

"It's time to escalate things. I want Cachar infantry uniforms for my men and I want those two recalled. I will need all hands to do what we need to do next."

Frances leaned forward excitedly, curiosity burning in his eyes.

"Oooh, do tell!"

Padu arrived and the interrogation of the prisoners began. They had been softened up by the forced march and had spent a painful interlude in a stress position. The officer was reluctant to start with, but the soldier was quite forthcoming. Their orders had been to infiltrate into Cachar and disrupt the supplies to the capital from the British-held territories. Take prisoners and bring them back for interrogation.

After a little more strenuous persuasion involving a board and buckets of water the officer confirmed what the soldier had told them and also gave up other information on troop movements within Assam. None of which told them anything they didn't already know.

When they were finished, they handed them over to the Cacharies who promptly executed them.

Sebastian arrived followed a day later by Antton. Both were dressed like locals and unshaved. They relished a hot bath and the ministrations of a barber before dressing in European clothes. They were called to a team briefing.

"That's better," Marty grinned as they walked into the room, "I thought you had both gone native on me."

"Tempting, their clothes are better suited to the climate," Sebastian said.

"You are probably wondering why I recalled you. Well. I want us to do something that will push the Burmese over the edge."

"Do tell," Sebastian said, intrigued.

Marty had a large map pinned up on the wall that showed the entire region. He indicated a spot on the border near a town called Moreh in the southeast and another in a forested area on the southern border.

"There are only two main roads that lead from Burma into Manipur, we cut them, and the Burmese will be mightily unhappy. The border follows rivers in both places here and here and has bridges that the Burmese have built to make crossing easier."

"What is the construction of the bridges?" Richard asked.

"Wooden trellis."

"Blow out the main supports then."

"Yes, and that could be done with the minimum of fuss, but that is not what I want. I want the explosions to be spectacular, loud and proud."

"Making a statement." Sebastian said.

"Indeed, and not only that, I want the blame to land squarely on the Cachar's shoulders," Marty added.

"When?" Frances asked.

"On the king's birthday."

"That is audacious," Frances said, "I like it. The king won't be able to ignore it and will have to let the war party have its way."

"I'm glad you like it, so you won't mind lending me Padu," Marty said.

The Bridges

The team's preparation was meticulous. The uniforms had to be adjusted to fit and concealed amongst packages of trade goods. Charges were made up and wrapped in oiled paper and fireworks made. Marty's vision had the bridges go up at the end of a spectacular fireworks show that would attract anyone in the area. He fully expected the Burmese to rebuild them in a couple of months if not weeks, but the statement was the important thing and the fact they were on the border.

To that end Rick Richard and Bert Smythe made Roman candles, giant ones. Two-inch diameter bamboo tubes were sealed at the end with clay. A biscuit of black powder that had been moistened and tamped down hard, placed at the bottom, then a layer of iron filings mixed with sulphur followed by another charge of loosely packed powder. Repeat until the three-foot tube was full. They sealed the top with a thin layer of clay with a fuse running through the middle of it.

They would split into two teams after crossing into Manipur further south from Mizoram where there was a ford across the River Tuival. Their cover story was that the fireworks were to celebrate the king's birthday. Two carts were needed to carry it all and Rick and Bert were given the task of driving them. "You made them, you carry them," Antton told them.

The brothers Singh were delighted at the thought of blowing up the bridges and fully supported the expedition. They even gave Marty the honorary rank of General and Sebastian and Antton the ranks of Major. Their uniforms were adorned with the insignia. However, they had to stay out of sight until they reached their objective, stealth and a low profile was what was needed now.

They travelled south disguised as traders. Darkened skin making them look like the natives they were dressed as. The fact that the carts were escorted by armed guards was enough to keep people away.

That changed after the border. Marty spoke Hindi and used forged travel documents crafted from old ones he had kept from the embassy and a permit saying they were to decorate the bridges with fireworks. A little judicious cleaning had enabled him to change the wording to give the groups permission to travel with their goods. However, the Burmese soldiers were greedy and demanded bribes to allow them to continue at every checkpoint.

They had little choice but to pay which was rapidly depleting their reserves of cash, so when they arrived at Singngat, Marty decided to replenish them.

Singngat was on a crossroads, the southern leg of which led to the southern border, and it was here the teams would split up. It was also the home of a large garrison and a regional governor who was Indian but working for the Burmese. He was hated by the locals and tolerated but disliked by the invaders. However, he didn't seem to care as he was getting rich from it. Marty decided it was time the fat bastard contributed to the rebellion.

The governor's house was set on a hill overlooking his domain. It was large, opulent, and guarded. But that never stopped a master thief. Marty and Matai entered the grounds over one of the high walls topped with spikes that surrounded the property. They easily avoided the two guards who only patrolled close to the house. Entry was simple for the two experienced housebreakers. They soon located the governor's bedroom and Matai dispatched him by cutting his throat. They searched his room and found a small fortune in gold and silver. Marty signalled they had enough and took a package from his shoulder bag. He set the timer and placed it under the bed. They left as quietly as they came and joined their colleagues at the place they were staying.

Just after dawn there was shouting from outside and they all went out to see what the fuss was about. They made sure they were seen. Up on the hill a huge column of smoke rose into the air as the governor's mansion burnt to the ground.

Sebastian, Bert, and their team headed south, Marty and the rest continued east. Sebastian had Padu take the role of the merchant while the rest were porters or guards. The bribes continued to flow but the permit kept them moving despite the attention of the soldiers.

Once they entered the hills and forests, they were more concerned with bandits. The army patrolled the roads regularly by cavalry, but they were well spaced out and the gaps gave ample opportunity for a bit of highway robbery. The men were on high alert.

Whether it was the visible display of guns or the patrols, they weren't bothered and made it to the bridge unmolested. Now they had to wait as the date set for the detonation was the twenty-third at noon and they had several days to wait before then to give Marty and his team a chance to get to their bridges.

They followed a trail upriver from the bridge to a point where they could make camp. All traces of their tracks were brushed out and the camp was set back in the trees and out of sight of the river, the trail, and the road. Sebastian went to the river and examined the bridge.

"It's a well-built bridge. Looks to be made of teak."

"No problem, we will make a nice display and then blow it to matchwood," Bert grinned.

Come the evening of the twenty-second they got to work.

Marty and his team had much further to go and had to push the horses to get there on time. The incident in Singngat was behind them and there seemed to be no repercussions as the patrols and check points were not any worse than before. It took them until the evening of the twenty-second to reach the bridge.

They quite openly attached the roman candles to the bridge's rails and the guards watched them curiously, but their permits said they were there to celebrate the king's birthday, so they left them alone. What the guards didn't see was Rick climbing down the trestle with a backpack full of charges.

Rick hummed quietly to himself as he tied the specially made charges to the supports. They were an innovation by the Toolshed to give more cutting power to the explosion. The charge was encased in an iron, square section trough, sealed at both ends and with a V-shaped copper insert sealing the open side. They had experimented and found the optimal thickness of metal to make the trough from and an intuitive guess had come up with the V-shaped copper insert that directed the charge. They were wrapped in cloth to prevent clinking.

All Rick had to do was strap the charges to the supports and link them with a fast fuse. This was another innovation. The fuse was wrapped in paper which increased the rate of burn tenfold and travelled at hundreds of feet per second. He happily did his work meticulously positioning and strapping the charges on the inside of the supports so they could not be seen from the road above.

By the time he placed the last on the second bridge it was past midnight, and he made his way up to the road to where the last roman candle was strapped to the rail. This one was special; it had a length of fuse that came out of its base that Marty had fixed to the back of the post ready for Rick to tie on to.

Attaching the fast fuse to that was simple but Rick made sure it was double secure. There would be no misfires on his watch.

Come midday the bridges were busy, and Marty asked the guards to clear them. They refused so he shrugged and walked away. Matai was waiting to light the fuse on that bridge and Antton at the other bridge as Marty stepped off the bridge, he shook his head. Marty kept walking and a guard chased after him. Shouting in Hindi.

"Are you going to start the celebration?"

"Do you want the honour?" Marty said.

The guard stopped dead with a smile on his face.

"Can I?"

"If you want, here take this." Marty handed him a striker. "When I fire my gun, light the fuse."

The guard looked like all his Christmases had come at once as he approached Matai who smiled and held up the end of the fuse.

Marty raised his pistol and fired into the air.

The guard took the striker and showered sparks onto the exposed end. After his third attempt it caught. The fuse shot along its length, dividing to light the fireworks on both sides of the bridge. Further along the river you could see the smoke from the other bridges display.

The display was magnificent and the soldiers chanted in praise of their king. Balls of sparks rose into the air as the candles fired their loads and the bangs echoed across the river valley.

Marty counted the shots as he and the boys retreated slowly to a safe distance. "One, two, three, four, five. Duck!"

The last shot of the last candles ignited the special fuse which ignited the fast fuses which burnt so quickly that you could hardly track them. The supports were cut from one end of the bridges to the other and they collapsed gracefully into the river taking anybody on them with them.

The guards on the Manipur side looked on in horror. The one who had lit the fuse stood eyes wide and mouth open. Antton slipped a knife between his ribs.

Marty shouted a rebel slogan and the rest of the boys opened fire killing all the guards on their side of the river. Cheering rose from the locals and several more guards were beaten to death.

They retreated to the town where they changed into the Cachar uniforms.

"We go out and kill any Burmese we see. We will be back here in an hour to get the hell out of town and into the countryside. Clear?" Marty said.

The men nodded and went out in pairs. Marty had Antton with him. They strutted through the town, rifles at the ready and a crowd of locals soon surrounded them, cheering and dancing. A squad of cavalry appeared and tried to force their way through the crowd to get to them. They waited until they started to raise their swords then opened fire taking the lead two out of their saddles. That was enough for the locals to turn on them and drag the rest from their saddles.

"Time to go," Marty said.

They changed personas, split into pairs, and avoided the roads as they retreated back towards the rendezvous with the other team and British controlled territory. It was a nervous journey, avoiding patrols and checkpoints, sleeping rough, or finding safe houses owned by trusted people. The Burmese and their collaborators were out on force searching for them once word got to the capital. It took longer to get back than to get there. But they all arrived at the rendezvous within a day.

Sebastian reported it all went well at the other bridge, and that, as it was secluded with no nearby towns, the effect on any locals had been minimal. They had put on their uniforms and sent a volley or two across the river to the guards on the far side to let them know who had done it.

They approached the border. The road was blocked on the Manipur side and a large contingent of soldiers manned the barrier. Marty examined the deployment of the troops and then across the gap to the other side where an equally large number of troops of the Bengal regiment were present along with a face he knew.

"They have closed the border. Looks like we might have to fight our way across. Our old friend Partho is there on the other side."

Sebastian had also been scanning the border.

"There are only five more of them than us, we have them outnumbered."

He was probably right, with their breech-loading rifles and revolvers they certainly out gunned them. Marty took out a mirror and flashed a signal at Partho who could hardly miss the light flashing directly into his face. He looked across at their position and nodded even though he couldn't actually see them.

"Get ready, we move in five minutes," Marty said. He wanted to get everybody home safe so was precise with his instructions.

'We move forward under rolling volley fire, once we are a hundred yards from them. As soon as we are within range we shift to pistols and grenades. The second rank will throw their grenades as soon as the first rank fire, after I give the command 'last volley'. Pado, you follow behind us."

The manoeuvre was well known to the lads who had practised and performed it a hundred times. Guns were prepared and reloads taken from satchels and put in belt pouches within easy reach. Pistol priming caps were checked and replaced if necessary.

The clock ticked down.

"Form up."

The men formed two ranks.

"Advance."

They were spotted and the Burmese soldiers formed up across the road, around half had muskets the rest bows. A hundred yards from them, the first rank dropped to a knee and aimed. Marty was in the middle and gave the order.

"First rank, fire!"

The rifles spat fire and smoke; their bullets sent spinning towards the enemy. As soon as they fired the second rank rushed forward to take up positions ten paces ahead.

Marty and his rank reloaded. It took them ten seconds.

"Second rank, fire!"

They moved forward through the smoke. An arrow clunked into the ground ahead of them. Shots were fired by the Burmese. The process was repeated eight more times until they were twenty yards away.

"Final volley!" Marty called.

Rifles were slung around on their straps, pistols drawn and cocked. Small black globes trailing smoke arced forward.

The grenades exploded and Marty yelled, "At them lads."

They charged forward and shot anyone who got in front of them. But the opposition was light. There were more bodies than active defenders. They didn't stop but ran straight across to the Indian side.

A puffing Marty stood in front of Partho, hands on his knees.

"You sailors are fucking unfit." Partho chuckled and slapped him on the back.

"Admiral Stockley?" a captain asked.

"The very same," Partho said.

The captain ignored him.

"Captain Earnest Kingsford, 2nd Battalion Bengal Regiment at your service. My men and I will escort you back to our headquarters. General Paget's orders."

"I hope you have horses. We left ours over there," Marty said.

Preparing for War

Marty sat in Frances' office in Calcutta. Cachar had become too dangerous for the spy master to stay there.

"My people report that the Burmese are rebuilding the bridges very quickly and are massing troops on the border to move into Manipur," Frances said.

"And from there to Assam by all accounts," Marty said.

"Yes, the rebellion there has gained enough momentum to warrant a move to subdue it. If they do that, we will get involved."

"There is still an opportunity to weaken the Burmese. They have to pass through the mountains in the north of Manipur to get to Assam. We could set up an ambush and thin them out a bit."

"Risky, the Burmese are at home fighting in the mountains and it's a long way home from there."

Marty harrumphed and slouched in his chair. He was itching to do something, and Frances knew it.

"What you need is a mission that doesn't take you all the way across Assam. This arrived from the admiralty yesterday." He handed over a packet of papers that had been opened.

"You opened a letter addressed to me?"

"You were not back then, and I wanted to see if it was anything important," Frances said with ingenuous innocence.

Marty gave him a sideways look and opened the letter.

"Hmm, they want me to take command of the East India Marine and in the case of war with Burma lead it to suppress their navy. This at the request of the Company commissioners." He checked the date. "Two months old."

"How did they know two months ago that I would be back now?" Marty asked him suspiciously.

"Um, I told Canning that at the rate things were developing you should be free around now."

"Really, and how did you know that?"

"It was an educated guess."

"Well, it looks like George had a word in the commissioner's ears then the first lord acted on it. How many ships of the Marine are in Calcutta?" Marty asked as most of their ships were in Bombay.

Frances dug around on his desk and came up with a sheet of paper. They have the Sloop HCS Aurora and a Brig HCS Vestal." He said it glumly, watching for Marty to explode.

"That's it?"

"Afraid so."

Marty did not react as Frances expected, instead, he pulled another letter from his coat pocket.

"What's that?"

"Oh, a letter from James Turner," Marty said as if butter wouldn't melt in his mouth and it was of no consequence.

Frances looked at him suspiciously.

"He told you all this in that letter, didn't he?"

"That and the fact that the SOF are on their way here and should arrive any day now."

Frances's eyes widened and his mouth opened and shut until he spluttered, "And you let me go in as if I was giving you the worst news!"

"Serves you right." Marty laughed.

The Special Operations Flotilla sailed into port two weeks later and were greeted by Marty and Wolfgang. Their ships needed some attention having come directly from the Mediterranean. Their bottoms were fouled, and their rigging needed replacement. Luckily the Company docks were ready to do the work at the Company's cost. They had four dry docks of sufficient size in Calcutta and the ships were soon being refitted with the Neaera hauled up on the careening beach.

James got time to spend with his family and especially Melissa, who almost fainted in shock when he walked in, as nobody had told her the flotilla had arrived. The only person who wasn't overjoyed was Sebastian.

"Cheer up, old man, it's not the end of the world," James said sitting beside the glum-looking soldier.

"It's alright for you. You and Melissa are back together again. Beth is still in South America."

"Oh, so that's the problem. Well go and see Father, he wants a word with you."

Sebastian found Marty in his office going over a pile of reports from the shipwrights in the yard on his ships.

"Ahh James found you, sit down I have some news," Marty said.

He looked worried and Sebastian feared the worst.

"You have been recalled along with Sir Raymond and Peter. You will all return to England on the fast packet. Which incidentally leaves Calcutta tomorrow afternoon." Marty's face split into a grin as he rose to shake Sebastian's hand.

Sebastian leapt to his feet and shook the offered hand.

"Do you know what comes next?"

"No, but I have recommended that you be given several months' leave."

Sebastian whooped.

"You should be able to cadge a lift on one of the Stockley ships when it makes the regular trip to Jamaica. Turner can tell you where Beth is. Here this letter will get you the passage."

That night Roland prepared a sumptuous feast, and the party went on late into the night. They gave the three men a right royal send-off which they had weeks to get over.

The captains of the two company ships reported to Martin at his home. McKinlay, the master and commander of the Aurora was a young Scot from Aberdeen, softly spoken but with steel in his eye. Bridger, the commander of the Vestal was older and a Somerset man.

"Gentlemen, welcome, please take a seat," Marty said as they entered. He was dressed in his working Admiral's uniform, but his coat was tossed over the back of a chair.

"May I say how pleased we are to have you in command Sir," McKinlay said. "I have heard of the times you were here in the past."

"Indeed," Marty said, "highly exaggerated, I am sure. Now you will be part of a newly formed squadron made up of your two ships and my flotilla which has arrived from the Mediterranean."

The two men nodded.

"My flag captain is Wolfgang Ackermann of the Unicorn, and he speaks with my voice. Understood?"

"Yes, Sir. Is he navy, Sir?" Bridger asked.

Marty gave him a straight look, "Not only navy but has more service years than the two of you put together. He is extremely experienced and has fought in these waters more than once."

Bridger looked slightly abashed but did not look away.

Marty got on with it,

"We will inspect your ships tomorrow at eight bells of the morning watch. I want full lists of crew, spares and stores. We will be at sea for an extended time so report any deficiencies or shortages and we will get them resolved.

"When was your last refit?"

"Four months ago," McKinlay reported.

"A year ago, her bottom needs cleaning," Bridger said.

"Report to the careening beach and get a slot. Give them this, it will speed things up." Marty scribbled a note and signed it before handing it over. "That is all."

He nodded to them and went back to his paperwork, which they correctly interpreted as a dismissal.

Marty and Wolfgang stepped onto the deck of the Aurora as the last two chimes of eight bells rang out. Both were in full uniform. They were met by a smart side party with young Commander McKinlay and his First, Champion Hardwyke.

Marty had read about Champion, who liked to be called Chappy. He was notorious as a fighter and had been in trouble a number of times during his career for wrecking bars and brawling. On the other hand, he was purported to be an excellent sailor and gunner. Marty shook his hand and noted the belligerent look in his eye and very firm grip.

"If you would proceed," Wolfgang said and pulled on a pair of white gloves.

Marty suppressed a smile; he had never known Wolfgang wear gloves on an inspection. They toured the main deck. Being a sloop, the Aurora had a single through deck. Marty and Wolfgang knew her of course as they had rescued her from the Marathas a few years before. Marty looked up at the mainmast.

"That's new, the old one had a ball embedded in it, about there."

Lieutenant Hardwyke stood beside him.

"It was replaced after she was recovered, Sir. I joined her then."

"Your predecessor is on the Leonidas as third."

"Allan is here?"

Marty ignored the lack of the sir.

"Yes, do you know each other?"

"We do, Sir, we grew up together."

"Make sure you look him up. He may keep you out of trouble."

The ships were in good condition, well organised and manned. A lot of the crew were former navy hands who had opted to stay in India after the war finished and were signed off. The lists were handed over and added to the already large pile of papers for his attention.

James and Melissa spent all the time he could spare together but Angus Fraser kept him busy with the refit. The Neaera was last to go into dock so they did as much of a refit on her upper works as they could before they got there. It was November before she was docked and the end of January before she came out.

Christmas was a time of balls and parties when everyone could forget there was a war brewing in the northeast. Adam and his new bride proudly announced she was pregnant which sent Caroline into a frenzy of preparation. Marty was more pragmatic.

"Do you want to stay here for the birth?"

"Will we sail soon then?"

"As soon as the Neaera is ready, she's due out in a month. We should be at sea by the end of February."

"Then I will be with you. Mima doesn't expect me to be there as that is not the custom in Burma."

"Caroline will take good care of her."

The second piece of news was that James and Melissa officially set their wedding date for October after the end of the monsoon season. India would be beautiful then as all the flowers and blossoms would be in full cry. Marty smiled as he thought about it and how busy Caroline would be organising it all while he was away.

The squadron was finally complete and Marty called an all-captains meeting on the Unicorn the morning that the governor announced that the British were at war with Burma.

"Gentlemen, I believe all the SOF captains have met and gotten to know our marine colleagues. This is one unified command which we are all part of. We have been designated as the Bengal Squadron and are officially part of the Company Marine for the records. I have negotiated with the Company, and they have agreed to honour the navy's rules for prizes."

That got a cheer from all the captains as the company was far less generous than the navy. Marty waited for the clamour to die down then continued.

"I have issued you all with the list of formations we will sail and expect you to be familiar with your position in them. We will rehearse them once we are at sea along with the usual exercises. We will be up against large well-armed junks that will be a challenge for the smaller ships. My proposal is that you hunt in pairs. The Nymph and the Aurora will be one pair, the Endellion and Vestal the second and the Neaera and Eagle the third. The frigates will be ready to support you if you find targets and will act independently. Any questions?"

"How will prizes be distributed around the squadron?" Hardwyke asked, causing grins from the SOF captains.

"All prizes are distributed across the squadron by the size of their crew whether the ship is in sight or not. From there, in each ship, in the usual navy ratios."

Hardwyke looked confused.

"Let me give you an example. We take prizes that net us £20,000 pounds in prize money. Take the total number of men in the squadron, which is around 1200 men and officers. Dividing £20,000 by 1200 gives us a single share of £16,14s. How many men are on your ship?"

"One hundred twenty, Sir."

"So, your ship's share would be 120 x £16,14s which equals £2,004."

Light dawned in his eyes.

"Good, you have it. Now one last thing. Hunting pairs are to stay in sight of the frigates at all times until you get the signal 'pursue'. That is all, now enjoy a drink and a toast to our success."

Adam came in with a tray of port and handed glasses around.

"Gentlemen, I give you the king."

"The king!" they all cried and downed their glasses to heel taps.

James Campbell stepped forward and raised his refilled glass. "Gentlemen, to success. Happy hunting!"

"Happy hunting!" the captains cried and drained their glasses again.

They went to sea. Cheered along the river out of Calcutta by a crowd of well-wishers. As they entered the Bay of Bengal, Marty felt a sense of freedom. The fresh air, cries of the birds and the sound of the ship settling in, to being at sea again. She creaked a little, the rigging hummed, and the sails fluttered as the men trimmed them. The age-old sound of feet pounding the deck, some shod, others bare. The bosun's calls and the lieutenants shouted orders.

He looked up at his admiral's pennant. White with the cross of Saint George and two bullseyes denoting him a Rear Admiral of the White. It was a long time coming but he knew he would be just as happy as a captain again.

Marty brought himself back to the present. "Wolfgang please have the squadron prepare to execute formation Beta."

Wolfgang gave the orders and signals flew up the lanyards. As they flew the preparatory, each ship acknowledged when they were ready.

"Execute," Marty barked.

The hunting pairs changed course and fanned out ahead of the frigates. The Nymph and Aurora set off to take station out to the north, the Endellion and Vestal dead ahead, with the Neaera and Eagle to the south. Each stayed in sight of the Unicorn's mainmast lookouts, hull up on the horizon. Marty went up for a look surprising the lookout who budged over to make room for him on the top gallant yard.

He scanned the horizon noting the position and deployment of the pairs. He was happy to see that each pair separated enough to maximise the amount of sea they could search.

Combat

Crossing the Bay of Bengal took forty-eight hours now that all the ships had nice clean bottoms. They started their patrol in the Andaman Sea. As they were close to the islands Marty called the hunters in to just two miles from the frigates.

"Signal the Endellion to take a look into Aerial Bay. It's a regular port for both pirates and the Burmese Navy," Marty said.

"Is there any difference?" Wolfgang said after giving the order.

"Difference between what?" Marty said.

"Pirates and the Burmese Navy."

"The navy has bigger guns."

Wolfgang laughed.

The Endellion acknowledged and peeled away from her station; her consort stayed put.

"We will circumnavigate the islands and check all the bays. If we find anything we will sink or burn it," Marty said.

The Endellion appeared as they came up to the bay. A puff of smoke indicated she had fired a gun. The report arrived moments later.

"She is signalling, 'Enemy in Sight'" reported Midshipman Woakes who was on signal duty.

"Bring the ship to action!" Wolfgang barked. "Signal formation alfa."

The Endellion came to hailing distance and Philip Trenchard reported that the ships were concentrated in the deep water to the south of the bay. Marty's plan was to sail in and serve the ships in the harbour broadsides as his ships passed. With the Eagle and Neaera staying behind to pick off any who made a run for it.

The hunters formed a line of battle, two cables apart with the frigates in the centre. The Nymphe and Aurora led, followed by the Unicorn and Leonidas, then Endellion and Vestal. The Eagle and Neaera swung out upwind to wait.

Some of the Burmese ships got the jump on them. As they rounded the island in the centre of the bay and turned west to start their run, several large junks were already making their way out. Marty could only presume that they had been ready to sail when the Endellion entered the harbour.

However, the entrance to the bay was less than a thousand yards wide which put the fleeing ships well within range of the main battery of the frigates.

"Engage!" Marty ordered and the sides of the Unicorn and Leonidas erupted clouds of smoke and flames. The first junk made it out and was immediately pursued by the agile Eagle who crossed her square stern and served her with her carronades. The Neaera focussed on the second junk, that was damaged, with her twelve-pound-longs.

One junk fired back hitting the Leonidas and wounding two men as a stone shot shattered on hitting the rail. James Campbell stood on his quarterdeck watching his well-drilled men reload. Out of habit he had his watch in his hand. *One minute fifteen seconds,* he noted happily. He saw that the loblolly boys retrieved the wounded men and took them below for the surgeon to attend to. He would check on them later.

On the Neaera, James Stockley was commanding the battery. The twelves were a good gun and could throw a ball at least two miles. Accurate, fast to load they suited the Neaera perfectly. They had gotten off the first broadside and now were preparing their second with loads of chain and bar.

The gun captains' hands raised, and James gave the order. The guns fired a rippled broadside starting from forward. Each of the eight guns barked in turn. The junk's rigging took a lot of damage, her sail fell, and the fore mast developed a distinct kink.

"Take us alongside and smash those oars. Marines ready!" Angus Frasier shouted.

James ordered the guns loaded with grape which was heavier than canister and more able to penetrate the hull. His gunners were ready just as the Neaera ground down the junk's side snapping her oars off.

"Fire as you bear," James shouted and pulled his pistols.

The grape smashed through the junk's thin hull and wrought devastation inside, but men still tried to fight from her deck. James aimed, fired, and missed his target, hitting another man on the crowded deck.

Swivel guns barked and the marines fired a volley before Angus ordered, "Boarders away!"

They left behind a burning hulk.

Marty was focussed on the ships in harbour. He counted fourteen, most of which were typical pirate junks. Three caught his eye. One was very large and ornate and flew a strange flag, the other two plainer but still decorated, rode beside her.

"Signal to all ships," he paused as he decided how to say what he wanted. "Bride and bridesmaids to be boarded intact." That was a hard one for the signaller. He had to spell it out, but he managed with the help of the fourth lieutenant.

Now all the gunnery practice came to the fore as each ship fired in succession.

"I want a boarding party to capture that floating brothel," Marty ordered.

"The bridesmaids as well?" Wolfgang asked.

"If you can manage it."

"Signal, 'all ships heave to'; emphasise with a red rocket.

Mr McGivern, I want boarding parties aboard those three ships."

More signals flew. The Leonidas's boats were brought into action and joined the Unicorn's heading to the junks. Marty rode in the last one at Wolfgang's insistence. He reached the side to a lot of screaming and shouting. A man ran past him holding his trousers up; a marine took aim and shot him with his rifle. Eventually peace was restored.

A small woman who was ornately dressed and made up was brought before him.

"Someone fetch Padu from the Unicorn, he will be down below somewhere."

Marty had requested Padu accompany them on the mission in case he needed to interrogate any prisoners. Now he sat on a convenient chair and waited.

Padu arrived and was helped aboard the flashy junk. Marty beckoned him over and asked him to translate.

"Who is she?"

"She is the madam of this brothel. "

Marty snorted a laugh; he had been right.

"Who owns it?"

"She was sent here by the king as a reward to the sailors."

There was a splash as a body was thrown overboard.

"Does the king own the ship?"

"No, it is the property of Dieng Chong We," Padu leant close to Marty, "he is a Chinese pirate."

"What is a Chinese pirate doing sending his floating brothel here for the king of Burma?"

The woman refused to say anymore.

A sweep of the ship evicted any remaining customers and rounded up the girls and crew who were bunched together on the main deck. The men also found two chests of coins and bullion, a fair amount of jewellery and a lot of spirits. Marty had those put under guard immediately.

"What to do with it? That is the question," Marty said to Wolfgang.

"Send it back to Calcutta then the company can decide."

"Then you had better select a prize crew of eunuchs if you want them to get there," Marty said, half seriously.

"There is that, and the impact the appearance of a floating brothel would have on our women."

Marty swore, he had not thought of that. They would all have to reassure their better halves that nothing had happened.

"Alright, that settles it, take everything of value off the ships, put the girls and the crew ashore and burn them."

Wolfgang gave one of his wolfy grins. "Very wise."

There was much wailing and crying as the crew and girls were put ashore. Most were Chinese with just a few Burmese and Javan. The plume of smoke from the burning ships could be seen for miles.

The circumnavigation of the island didn't bring much. They sank a couple of armed junks but apart from that there were just fishing boats.

"Take us to Yangon," Marty ordered as he wanted a look into the estuary.

They sailed in beta formation to the Gulf of Martaban and again sent in the Endellion for a reconnaissance. The Eagle captured a cargo boat full of rice and the Aurora captured a pair of medium-sized junks carrying teak and rice.

"Could we blockade the port?" McGivern asked while they waited.

"We could but all they have to do is re-route their ships through the delta which is impossible to blockade. It might be worth leaving the sloops here though, to gather up as many prizes as they could."

The sound of a cannon attracted their attention. Marty took up a telescope and looked towards the mouth of the river. He chuckled. The Endellion was running before four large junks who were using sail and oars to try and overtake her.

"Oh, that is rich. Philip is leading them a chase, making just enough sail to keep ahead of them."

"Signal, 'Enemy sighted,' and 'Engage'."

The Unicorn was already at quarters. Wolfgang ordered topsails and gallants set, the jibs taken in, to clear the arc of fire for the forward carronades.

The junks were only a mile away when they broke off their chase seeing the squadron bearing down. They were too late. The outlying ships had swung in behind them cutting off their retreat.

The Endellion spun on her heel with a manoeuvre straight out of the racing yacht handbook. It took excellent seamanship on the part of the captain and crew to turn that fast and that tight through the wind. She beat the junks to the turn by a country mile and her carronades were put into action at close range.

"Damn that was some fine sailing!" Marty exclaimed.

"I taught him everything he knows." Wolfgang laughed at his own joke.

Marty gave him a quick glance; Wolfgang did not joke, normally. The Unicorn was beaten to the junks by the Eagle, Vestal, and Aurora who set about them with a will. The Nymphe, Unicorn, Neaera and Leonidas closed in, and when it was all over and they had a string of five prizes.

Marty called another all-captains meeting.

"Gentlemen, we have done well so far but there is more to be done. The Nymphe, Vestal and Aurora will maintain station here in the Gulf to pick off prizes and to keep a watch for any large formations of ships leaving Yangon. One of you must be in sight of the Yangon River estuary at all times."

"Sir, may I ask. If we have prizes, what should we do with them?" Andrew Stamp said.

"Do not take so many as to deplete your crews below fighting strength. The Endellion and Eagle will act as our messenger ships and will visit regularly. They will escort any prizes back to Calcutta. Work up rendezvous points and contingencies between you and give them to Trevor and Philip," Marty replied.

Marty pointed to a chart pinned to a board on an easel.

"This is Shaipuri Island. The Burmese have occupied it, but it belongs to the Company. We will take it back."

He pinned up a larger scale map of the area.

"As you can see, the island is in fact the end of the Teknaf Upazila peninsula cut off by a narrow channel. The River Naf is the border between Bengal and Burma here on the east side. It is surrounded by beaches which make it perfect for an amphibious landing. Angus and James will land the marines from the Neaera supported by the guns of the Unicorn and Leonidas. I am told that the island is quite heavily wooded, Declan, so you should prepare your marines accordingly."

"Half of them are woodsy so they will be right at home," Declan said dryly, making them laugh.

The squadron separated and the main group headed north. They passed Manaung and Ramree Islands which they had cleaned out a few years before. Marty had the Endellion take a look into the channel behind the island but there was no sign of pirates.

Shaipuri Island was just as the chart showed it. It was relatively flat, wooded with scattered settlements. A scouting mission by the Unicorn's cutter discovered that the Burmese had crossed the river and taken the island using river boats. The only fortification they saw was a wooden palisade enclosing the army camp, some seven hundred yards from the east beach.

Marty and Declan O'Driscoll decided a night landing was possible on the west side to get their men in position for a dawn advance to push the Burmese into the sea. The Leonidas would sail up the west side and the Unicorn and Neaera the west to the landing beach. The two frigates would pound the camp with their main guns.

All their marines were transferred to the Neaera along with contingents of sailors who would support them on shore with swivel guns and mortars. It made for an uncomfortable night on the brig, and they were all grateful when the order to bring the landing barges around to the leeward side was given.

James commanded the barges and put into operation their well-rehearsed landing procedure. The first three barges came up to the side and the marines climbed down cargo nets slung over the side to fill them ten to a barge. Once full they moved forward and the second set of three barges took their places.

Lamps on the stern of the barges allowed the cox's to form a line which advanced to the beach. As the barges had punt-like prows they simply ran up onto the sand and the marines exited over the bow. Once empty they returned to the Neaera to collect the next sixty men.

In this way a hundred and twenty marines and sailors were ashore and formed up in less than an hour. Captain Declan O'Driscoll led them supported by Lieutenant Alexander Beaumont, Colour Sergeant Bright and Sergeant Anfield. It was thirty minutes until dawn.

The sun rose and the Unicorn fired the first broadside of the attack. Balls crashed down on the camp smashing the palisade and wreaking havoc amongst the huts of the soldiers. The Leonidas joined in and the joint battery of some forty pieces roared out their challenge.

James was ashore commanding their man portable artillery with Dennis at his side. Dennis was a very large, extremely strong man who had the mind of a seven-year-old. He was born with a condition known as Mongolism at that time and later as Downs Syndrome. He was fiercely loyal to James who was the only person who had any influence or control over him at all. Dennis carried an over-large cutlass in his left hand and a boarding pike in his right. One thing Dennis enjoyed above all else was a good fight beside James.

The double line of marines advanced inland towards the camp, bayonets fixed and glinting in the morning sun. Their scarlet uniforms with their stark white cross belts looking like blood.

They neither shouted or sang, but advanced silently into the trees towards the camp, the balls from the Unicorn howling over their heads. After four broadsides the frigates fell silent.

The marines marched steadily on until they came to the edge of the large clearing where the camp was located. Declan walked forward and examined it. The palisade was breached in a number of places and the Burmese soldiers were busily trying to patch them up. James stepped up beside him.

"Mortars, I think, covering our charge to get inside. Walk them forward from the palisade and we will advance behind them. Once we are at the palisade bring your men up in support," Declan said.

James touched the brim of his hat in salute and went to give the orders. His men, a mixture of specialist marines and sailors set up the tubes on their stands while he calculated the declination to drop a bomb on the palisade from the manual.

"Twenty degrees should do it from here."

The first salvo was fired.

"Short by ten feet. Set them to twenty-two then drop three degrees every round."

The mortars fired with a regular thump, sending their deadly bombs to the enemy. After the third round the marines advanced. At the fifth, they charged.

"Cease fire, up and at them, lads!" James cried. The sailors howled as they charged, cutlasses and boarding pikes glittering wickedly in the sun. They clambered through the breaches and over bodies." The marines were ahead of them in square, firing volley after volley into a mass of screaming Burmese that surrounded them.

"Bring up the swivels!" James ordered. Dennis came up with one held like a shotgun.

"Who me shoot?" he said with a lopsided grin as he had a slow match between his teeth.

"Those heathens over there," Marty said and pointed.

Dennis held the gun against his hip one handed and touched the slow match to the touch hole.

"Bang you dead!" he laughed after the smoke cleared and he was reloading.

James shook his head. The men on either side had set their swivels mounted on poles and grinned at him.

The effect on that side of the square was instant. The Burmese finding themselves in a crossfire, turned and charged the sailors.

I didn't expect them to do that!

James fired his rifle and pulled his pistols firing shot after shot. He replaced them with his sword and knife as the first man reached him. Parry and cut, thrust, and stab. He bent to his work with a will, Dennis beside him stabbing with his pike and slashing with the cutlass.

James noticed another officer uniform beside him and glanced over to see his father with Hector beside him. Marty had come over after the barrage had ended and brought the Shadows with him along with more sailors. It was just as well, as they had underestimated the size of the garrison by a fair margin.

Suddenly with a roar the marines broke out of their square and attacked with bayonets. It seemed to James that the entire compound was a mass of hand-to-hand fighting. Men screamed war cries and others screamed in pain. He was busy, the Burmese soldiers were well trained and fought bravely.

In the end the British prevailed and the fighting ground to a halt. They took over a hundred prisoners with two hundred dead and dying. Wounded marines were helped back to the boats by their comrades, the dead carried with respect for burial at sea.

"Are you hurt?" Marty asked James.

"No, none of the blood is mine. Where is Dennis?"

"Over there carrying wounded men back to the boats."

Dennis was gently cradling a wounded marine in his arms, carrying him without obvious effort.

"One minute a howling murderer and the next as gentle as a lamb." James wondered, not for the first time.

"Admiral!" Lieutenant Beaumont called as he ran towards Marty across the compound.

"I just found out there is a second compound on the north coast."

Marty puffed out his cheeks. "How do you know that?"

"Padu interrogated a Burmese officer. He told us."

"Find Captain O'Driscoll, this isn't over yet."

Declan arrived and saluted.

Marty asked, "How are your marines?"

"Three dead, seven wounded but the rest are pretty chipper."

"Fit enough for another fight?"

"After a night's rest they will be."

"Able to march a mile?"

"That they can do."

"We will come back here and clean up later. Get them moving north."

Marty beckoned James over. "Get the ships and boats moved north a mile. There is a second compound. I will light a smoky fire three hundred yards due south of it so the Unicorn can bombard it. I will set up a chain of signallers with flags to guide their shooting.

The compound was much smaller than the first. The palisade was lined with men. *Forewarned is forearmed,* Marty estimated there were probably between fifty and a hundred. He organised the signallers. Three were sufficient and he sent his first message after he had the fire lit.

"One round for ranging and direction."

A boom echoed across the treetops and a ball plunged to ground a hundred yards long and fifty yards south. A correction was sent.

"Boom." The ball landed inside the palisade.

Another correction.

"Boom." A chunk of palisade was smashed to matchwood.

He was about to order them to fire for effect when the gates opened, and a Burmese officer walked out. Marty gathered Padu and the Shadows and walked towards him, meeting him halfway. The compound had surrendered. They only had sixty men and the eighteen-pound shot crashing through their camp had convinced them it was a lost cause.

Blockade

Once the island had the Company flag comfortably flying over it, Marty messaged Calcutta for a garrison of troops to secure it. A ship full of seasick Sepoys with a British officer arrived a week later. Some kissed the ground as soon as they came ashore.

"Rough passage?" Marty asked the major as he walked up the beach towards him.

"First time this lot have been on a ship. It was a bit choppy in the middle but other than that fairly calm. Major Howard Finlay 7th Madras." He held out his hand and Marty shook it.

"Martin Stockley, Admiral Royal Navy. As soon as you are installed, we are off."

"Did you have much trouble taking it?"

"A bit, there were more of them than we anticipated. Come I will show you the camp."

Marty told him about the fight on the walk to the main camp. The marines and sailors were repairing the palisade and making it more practical to defend.

"A ditch in front of it would improve it immensely," Finlay said.

"That will get your Sepoys over their seasickness."

"How many prisoners did you take?"

"One hundred and sixty give or take. They are locked up in the other camp."

"Well, I have one hundred and twenty men plus cooks."

"Any artillery pieces?"

"Oh, no. We are infantry."

"Then I will leave you ten swivel guns and ammunition. They should be enough to suppress any thoughts of escape if you mount them on the palisade pointing down into the camp."

The marines trained the Sepoys on the swivel gun and a week later they left with a promise to call in when they were passing. Their patrol would take them up to Chittagong and down to Yangon. Going north they didn't expect to see any Burmese ships but south would be a different matter.

Down in the Andaman Sea, Andrew Stamp and his three ships were patrolling off Bilu Island, behind which lay the city of Mawlamyine. It was one of the largest cities in Burma and a port. The island effectively sheltered the city and gave ships a choice of how to exit the Thanlwin River. They could go east around the north of the island or south along the river's southerly branch.

His ships were in an arc with the Vestal to the north and far enough out to sea to keep the Gulf of Martaban in sight and the Aurora to his south to watch the southerly exit from behind the island.

They had been on patrol for two days and already had a prize. The large cargo junk was tagging along behind the Nymphe like a duckling. An ugly one, but a duckling none the less.

"Vestal is signalling, 'Enemy in Sight'," a lookout hailed.

"Tell her to engage," Andrew said, standing orders were to only signal when there was a worthwhile prize and to just sink anything less.

"She is signalling 'Assist'."

"Make all sail. Signal the Aurora to maintain station."

The sails boomed as they dropped and filled with the wind. The Nymph accelerated.

"Make for the Vestal," Andrew ordered.

Andrew had grown a beard which the crew thought made him look piratical. He knew it and played the part.

"Action stations, me hearties!" he shouted in a fair impersonation of Marty's Dorset accent.

The crew responded and the ship was cleared for action in less than ten minutes. The Vestal was heading north.

"Can you see what she is chasing?" Andrew called up to the lookouts.

"Just a sail on the horizon so far, Sir."

Must be more than one, that brig could take anything the Burmese have one on one.

"Mr Hart, would you oblige me and take a glass up to the top gallant yard and see what we are up against."

"Aye, aye, Skipper."

He was gone before Andrew could chide him for the lack of a sir or captain. But he didn't really mind, being in the SOF was more relaxed than the navy and they were often asked to pose as civilian ships.

"Two war junks trying to chase the Vestal off by the looks of things, Captain," Stanley called down. "The Vestal is engaging them now."

The Vestal was armed with twenty twelve-pound-longs and would prefer to fight at range and pound her enemy into submission. The Nymphe was armed with fourteen, thirty-six-pound carronades and two twelve-pound-longs and preferred to get close in.

"Load small ball over ball in the carronades, ball in the twelves."

That would be a devastating load close up and he intended to get within a cable before firing. They were making twelve knots, and the Vestal was moving the fight closer to them. Still, it would be at least thirty minutes before they were in range.

Andrew had learnt patience. Nothing happened at sea faster than it did, so he would prepare his ship as well as he could for the inevitable destruction to come. He walked along the deck, exchanging greetings with his men and checking their readiness. He took a cutlas from the tub on the centreline where they were stowed until needed. It was razor sharp and free of rust.

He got back to the quarterdeck as they got to a mile. "Ready the twelves, let's announce our arrival."

At a three quarters of a mile, "Swing her bow to port to give the starboard twelve a shot."

Stanley was in charge of the guns and was ready for this.

"Fire as you bear. On the up roll!"

The gun belched fire and smoke. Andrew could see the black dot of the ball flying away from them.

"Close but it is going to miss," he said to the helm. "Swing her to starboard."

The port gun fared better, his ball crashed into the port bow of one of the junks at just below deck height sending a shower or splinters flying.

The Vestal which had been sailing away from the junks turned to engage them head on.

"Here we go, fire as you bear!"

At a cable, the carronades lived up to their reputation as smashers. The balls travelling at one thousand six hundred feet per second smashed timbers and bodies equally, making up for their low velocity with momentum and mass. Their short (under four feet) length made them easy to reload and by the time the last one fired, the first was already spouting its second load of death and destruction.

The Nymphe didn't get it all her own way. The Burmese got off a broadside and several men were wounded by splinters or stone fragments. But the British ship's superior armament, manoeuvrability and training made them more than a match for the junks which were outsailed and outgunned.

"Five prizes to take to Calcutta," Andrew told Trevor Archer when the Eagle came alongside. "What's been happening with the rest of the squadron?"

"We took back Shaipuri Island. Was a good little fight by all accounts. The Company sent a company of infantry to hold it. The boss thinks as long as there is a visible squadron passing by regularly the Burmese will not attack again."

"Uff, blockade work. Not what the SOF was meant for."

"Apparently the navy is sending out more ships to patrol the bay so we shouldn't have to do it for long."

"No change in our orders then?"

"No, you have to stay here and keep making us money." Trevor laughed.

"Just keep bringing back my prize crews and we shall." James shook his hand and Trevor went back to the Eagle.

By the time the Unicorn and her consorts re-joined the Andaman Sea unit, the supply of prizes had all but dried up. The mere sight of a sail was enough to send Burmese traders scuttling back into port. The Burmese Navy didn't have the firepower to dislodge them, and it turned into a stalemate. Marty took the Unicorn back to Calcutta to have a talk with Frances.

"When are the navy reinforcements due to arrive?" Marty asked.

"Three months at the earliest. They are bringing more troops out with them," Frances replied.

"Don't the Company have enough?"

Frances walked over to the map on his wall. "Cachar was a simple operation. We pushed the Burmese out fairly quickly. Assam is harder, the terrain is hilly to mountainous as you know, and the Burmese are excellent mountain fighters. We attacked in March and to date we have progressed from the border to a line at Nongstoin which is where it gets hilly. Progress has slowed and we are having to fight for every foot."

"Messy."

"Exactly, this is going to be a costly war in men and money. Talking of which, how is the rape of Burmese maritime trade fairing?"

"Almost dried up. They refuse to come out of port. We have dropped the blockade back, so our ships are less visible, but they have taken to hopping along the coast. Our boys are raiding coastal towns to entertain themselves."

"Shame but look at the bright side, you have made a fair amount of prize money already."

Marty started rotating ships back to Calcutta to give the crews some shore time. He also organised regular supply ships to be sent to the Andaman Sea to keep the squadron stocked with fresh food. Caroline, Melissa, and the wives made sure that their men's personal supplies were well catered for.

The months dragged by, and they now knew what the poor bastards on the channel blockade in the war must have felt like. Then the monsoons came and the winds in the Bay of Bengal and the Andaman Sea reversed. The weather was bad and got worse until in October the acute low-pressure area over northwest India shifted out to sea forcing the squadron back to Calcutta.

A rather battered squadron of ships tied off at the docks in Calcutta. In the pool ahead of them was a small fleet of British warships with the eighty-four gun two-deck Ganges flying a commodores pendant.

Marty grinned as he ordered the commodore to report aboard. He was the ranking officer after all. A tall man in an immaculate uniform walked down the dock to the Unicorn's gangplank. The side party that greeted him was equally immaculate and he was shown to the admiral's cabin.

"Commodore Quigley, Sir," the marine guard announced.

The deck beams of a frigate were much lower than the ones in an eighty-four and required Quigley to duck. Marty gestured for him to take a seat.

"Stay there and preserve your skull. We can't have the new commander knocking himself out," Marty said.

"Most considerate, Admiral. I have your orders here."

Marty took the packet and slit the seal with his fighting knife which was laying on his desk.

"I'm to return to Portsmouth with my ships and get a refit." He didn't tell Quigley why, which was also in the letter.

"I hear the war is much more difficult than first expected," Quigley said.

"Indeed, Paget underestimated the capabilities of the Burmese, especially in mountain warfare. This is not going to be over quickly." Marty briefed the commodore on the situation in the Bay of Bengal and Andaman Sea. When he finished, he invited him to dinner at the house.

The commodore asked if he could bring someone, and Marty expected him to bring his flag captain and was surprised when he turned up at the door with a very pretty Indian girl.

"This my wife, Nera. We met in Bombay the last time I was here in India to collect the Ganges from the yard in '82. We married a year later."

Then Marty remembered, the Ganges was a Bombay yard ship built of teak. Thirty-two twenty-fours on the upper deck, twenty-eight thirty-two-pounders and a pair of sixty-eight-pound carronades on the gundeck. A mix of twenty-fours and carronades on the quarter and foredecks. A formidable ship and quick, being almost one hundred and ninety-four feet long with a beam of fifty-two feet at the gundeck, the hull long and narrow.

"They are both beautiful," Marty said.

"Martin! You cannot place a woman and a ship in the same sentence," Caroline chided.

"Why not?" Marty teased. "We are both blessed with beautiful intelligent wives and our mistresses are our ships."

Caroline rolled her eyes and held up her hands in surrender. *Men and their ships.*

They would not leave until the monsoon passed in October. They might, with fair winds and good luck, be home in time for Christmas. However, Marty didn't get time off.

Frances visited the house and the two were walking through the garden.

"I've got a job for you."

"What is it?" Marty said.

"We need a certain individual to disappear."

"Why can't you handle that locally?"

"Because he is a senior British official."

Marty stopped and looked at Frances in surprise.

"We are taking out our own?"

"In this case, yes. He is a particularly unsavoury fellow, and he has a deep interest in keeping Burma out of the Company's hands."

Marty knew who he meant.

"Illingworth."

"The very same."

"I know about his business interests, but what makes him unsavoury?"

"He has bad manners and stinks."

"Not a reason to kill him."

"He is feeding information to the Burmese through his agents in Burma."

"Aah, now that is a good reason, but I still don't know why you don't just arrest him?"

Frances stopped walking and examined a rose.

"He is very well connected politically and this needs to be handled delicately."

"Alright, how do you want it handled?"

"It would be a terrible shame if his ship was to sink with him on it."

"Does he go sailing often?"

"Once a month he tells everyone he is going down to Madras when in fact he visits his factor in Burma."

Marty checked out Illingworth's ship, the Jekhane. It was a typical trader, ten guns which were in poor condition and under crewed. Illingworth bustled up the gang plank and shouted for the skipper to get moving. He went directly below.

The ship warped out from the dock, he would not pay for her to be towed, and set sail down river. The crew a scruffy lot, the dregs of the dockside. The sweet smell of opium smoke drifted up through the skylight of the main cabin.

The Jekhane entered the Bay of Bengal and was well out to sea before the skipper went down to the cabin. The smell of opium was strong, and he opened the transom windows to let the smoke out. Illingworth was sprawled on the cot, his eyes glazed.

Marty shook his head, searched the room, and threw any opium he found out of the window along with the pipes used to smoke it.

Illingworth came to as the effects of his last pipe wore off. He sat up, the ship was rocking and rolling in a very strange fashion. Something was banging regularly. He got off the cot and went into the cabin. The door was open and swinging with the roll. That was what was banging.

He went up on deck. The sails hung limp; the ship was drifting. He looked to the quarterdeck. There was no one there. The tiller swung back and forth unmanned. He stumbled along the deck, tripping on ropes and other detritus.

There was no one there.

He called out.

No one answered,

The rolling was getting worse.

He spotted an open hatch and looked down into the hold. It was half full of water that sloshed back and forth but it was what floated in it that made him gasp.

The skipper and crew's bodies sloshed back and forth with the water. The skipper, on his back, throat cut, gazed up at him from a swollen face.

Illingworth screamed, but there was no one to hear him. The horizon was clear, and no ships could be seen. He staggered down to his cabin but there was water sloshing over the floor already. He searched frantically for his opium and was still searching when the ship slipped below the waves.

Marty met Frances for lunch at the Calcutta Savoy.

"Illingworth's ship has been posted as missing in this morning's paper," Frances said.

"Has it? How overdue is it?"

"Two weeks now. No one is surprised, it was a bit of a wreck."

"Everyone assumes it sunk?"

"That's the popular opinion."

Frances took a sip of wine.

"How did you do it?"

"Do what?" Marty smiled.

Epilogue

Before they left there was the small task of getting James and Melissa married. Caroline had a wonderful time helping Melissa choose her gown and organising the event. Marty took James and Angus, who would be his best man, to a renowned tailor and got them brand-new lieutenant's uniforms made to measure. They also visited a goldsmith and had rings made of eighteen carat gold.

The ceremony would take place at Saint John's Cathedral. Built in 1787 it was a spectacular building with a large stately portico leading into a column lined nave lit by stunning stained-glass windows.

Caroline had invitations printed and invited the great and the good along with James' brother officers and the crew of the Neaera. The wedding breakfast would be at the Savoy.

James complained that it was all too much fuss and was reminded, firmly, that his social rank required it.

The day of the ceremony arrived, and the cathedral was decorated with flowers. James arrived with Angus and made his way to the altar. He was very nervous. Melissa arrived escorted by Caroline who as her guardian took the place of her mother and Marty who would give her away. They were five minutes late.

Melissa was dressed in an ivory silk dress with gold braiding and embroidery, her hair elaborately arranged with flowers and curled to hang over her left shoulder. She looked stunning of course.

James lost his nerves as soon as he saw her and admitted afterwards the whole thing passed in a blur. Marty granted him leave for a honeymoon touring India. They would return on a Company ship when that was over.

Quinten Stirling was made acting lieutenant and replaced him on the Neaera.

The household was packed and everything and everybody loaded onto the ships. The Pride took most of the baggage, including a new bed and the majority of the servants. Marty, Caroline, Adam, and Mary sailed on the Unicorn.

The relationship between Wolfgang and Mary had become plain to see when they had been ashore. He had walked her out many times and she obviously doted on him. So, it was no surprise when Wolfgang approached Marty when they were in international waters.

"Wolfgang," Marty said by way of greeting, as his flag captain walked to the rail where he was standing. Marty noted that there was not another man in listening distance.

"Martin." There was a long pause.

"I have a request."

"Yes?" Marty had an inkling what he wanted but wasn't about to make it easy for him.

"Mary and I have been stepping out now for quite some time and we would like to make the arrangement permanent."

"Congratulations."

Wolfgang frowned.

"We wish to get married as soon as possible."

"There is a wonderful chapel at Portsmouth," Marty said with a happy smile. Wolfgang looked at him in exasperation.

"Martin, we wish to get married at sea!"

"Oh! You want me to tie you two together."

"Not how I would have put it, but yes."

"Why didn't you say so! Of course, I would."

"I…" Marty grabbed his hand and slapped him on the back.

"You can get it blessed in Portsmouth," Marty grinned.

They were sailing between Ceylon and Reunion and the crew went to town decorating the ship. Not a single man stayed below when the ceremony was performed and the cheer that went up was followed by a seven-gun salute from the entire flotilla.

Mary moved into Wolfgang's cabin.

The ship settled back into its normal routine after that. Marty enjoyed the regularity of it all. He had had quite enough excitement for the time being.

The war would take two years to win and cost a lot of lives on both sides. Fifteen thousand died on the British side of which seventy-five percent of the Europeans died of disease. Over three thousand Indians were killed. Although there was never an official figure for the number of Burmese killed it is estimated to have been at least twenty thousand.

It ended in a decisive British victory giving them control over Assam, Manipur, Cachar, Jainita, Arakan Province and Tennasserim. The Burmese had to pay a million pounds in war reparations at the end of it which crippled their economy and led to the second and third wars.

Historic Notes

In the 18th century, the invention of the thermometer and barometer allowed for more accurate measurements of temperature and pressure, leading to a better understanding of atmospheric processes. This century also saw the birth of the first meteorological society, The Royal Society for the encouragement of Arts, Manufactures and Commerce (later Royal Society of Arts) in London in 1754, which helped popularise the science of meteorology. [Wikipedia]

Caipirinha is Brazil's national cocktail, made with cachaça (sugarcane hard liquor), sugar, and lime. The drink is prepared by mixing the fruit and the sugar together, then adding the liquor. This can be made in a single large glass to be shared among people, or in a larger jar, from which it is served in individual glasses. *(Wikipedia)*

Traditional ship builders use copper nails and roves to fix the hull planks to the frames. A square-shanked copper nail is driven through a pre-drilled hole in the plank and frame and as it emerges a rove, (a concave copper washer with a round hole) is placed over it and held in place with a rove punch while the nail is driven fully home. This is a real case of a square peg in a round hole. Once the nail is fully home, the point is snipped off and the end peened over like a rivet.

Burma in the early 19th century before the Anglo Burmese war had different names for the cities, Yangon instead of Rangoon, Pyay instead of Prome, Thayet instead of Thayetmyo. I use the traditional names for cities, not the colonial ones. Similarly, Ava in this book is now known as Inwa and at the time that Marty and Co arrived in Burma was the capital.

Suplex (plural suplexes) A wrestling move in which the wrestler picks up their opponent off the ground (or mat) and then, using a large portion of their own body weight, drives the opponent down on the mat by throwing them over their centre of gravity, usually arching their back.

Casus Belli is an act or an event used to justify a war.

Under the **pounds, shillings, and pence** (old money) system in the UK, instead of 100 pence in the pound, there were 20 shillings in a pound. There were 12 pence in a shilling. So, there were 240 pence in a pound. (Wikipedia)

- £1 = 20 shillings
- 1 shilling = 12 pence
- £1 = 240 pence

A Guinea was 21 shillings.

Marriage at sea In the early 18th century the marriage ceremony could be as simple as jumping over a broom and was official as long as it was registered in the parish rolls. Similarly, one could be married at sea and register the wedding in the ship's log, getting it blessed in a church was an option that many would take.

Glossary of sailing terms used in this book

Beam – The **beam** of a ship is its width at its widest point

Bowsprit – a spar projecting from the bow of a vessel, especially a sailing vessel, used to carry the headstay as far forward as possible.

Cable – a cable length or length of cable is a nautical unit of measure equal to one tenth of a nautical mile or approximately 100 fathoms. Owing to anachronisms and varying techniques of measurement, a cable length can be anywhere from 169 to 220 metres, depending on the standard used. In this book we assume 200 yards.

Cay – a low bank or reef of coral, rock, or sand especially one on the islands in Spanish America.

Futtock shrouds – are rope, wire or chain links in the rigging of a traditional square-rigged ship. They run from the outer edges of a top downwards and inwards to a point on the mast or lower shrouds, and carry the load of the shrouds that rise from the edge of the top. This prevents any tendency of the top itself to tilt relative to the mast.

Gripe – to tend to come up into the wind in spite of the helm.

Ketch – a two-masted sailing vessel, fore-and-aft rigged with a tall mainmast and a mizzen stepped forward of the rudderpost.

Knee – is a natural or cut, curved piece of wood.[1] Knees, sometimes called ships knees, are a common form of bracing in boatbuilding.

A Nautical Mile is 1.151 statute miles or 1/60th of a degree of latitude at the equator.

Leeway – the leeward drift of a ship i.e. with the wind towards the lee side.

Loblolly boys – Surgeon's' assistants

Lugger – a sailing vessel defined by its rig using the lug sail on all of its one or several masts. They were widely used as working craft, particularly off the coast. Luggers varied extensively in size and design. Many were undecked, open boats. Others were fully decked.

Mizzen – 1. on a yawl, ketch or dandy the after mast.
 2. (on a vessel with three or more masts) the third mast from the bow.

Pawls – a catch that drops into the teeth of a capstan to stop it being pulled in reverse.

In ordinary – vessels "in ordinary" (from the 17th century) are those out of service for repair or maintenance, a meaning coming over time to cover a reserve fleet or "mothballed" ships.

Ratlines – are lengths of thin line tied between the shrouds of a sailing ship to form a ladder. Found on all square-rigged ships, whose crews must go aloft to stow the square sails, they also appear on larger fore-and-aft rigged vessels to aid in repairs aloft or conduct a lookout from above.

Rib – a thin strip of pliable timber laid athwarts inside a hull from inwale to inwale at regular close intervals to reinforce its planking. Ribs differ from frames or futtocks in being far smaller dimensions and bent in place compared to frames or futtocks, which are normally sawn to shape, or natural crooks that are shaped to fit with an adze, axe or chisel.

Sea anchor – any device, such as a bucket or canvas funnel, dragged in the water to keep a vessel heading into the wind or reduce drifting.

Shrouds – on a sailing boat, the shrouds are pieces of standing rigging which hold the mast up from side to side. There is frequently more than one shroud on each side of the boat. Usually, a shroud will connect at the top of the mast, and additional shrouds might connect partway down the mast, depending on the design of the boat. Shrouds terminate at their bottom ends at the chain plates, which are tied into the hull. They are sometimes held outboard by channels, a ledge that keeps the shrouds clear of the gunwales.

Stay – is part of the standing RIGGING and is used to support the weight of a mast. It is a large strong rope extending from the upper end of each mast.

Sweeps – another name for oars.

Tack – if a sailing ship is tacking or if the people in it tack it, it is sailing towards a particular point in a series of lateral movements rather than in a direct line.

Tumblehome – a hull which grows narrower above the waterline than its beam.

Wear ship – to change the tack of a sailing vessel, especially a square-rigger, by coming about so that the wind passes astern.

Weather Gauge – sometimes spelled weather gage is the advantageous position of a fighting sailing vessel relative to another. It is also known as "nautical gauge" as it is related to the sea shore.

And now --

An extract from Lady Bethany Book 1
Spy School

The academy was a stately home in Coleshill, a village in the county of Berkshire. It was designed by Inigo Jones in the 17th century and was a mixture of Dutch, Greek, French and English architecture. It was perfect for training agents as it was secluded and owned by Baron Pleydell-Bouverie whose seat was at Longford Castle in Wiltshire, meaning he had little use for it. Being friends with George Canning it was natural for him to make the house available for the academy.

It had ample bedrooms, bathrooms, and reception rooms. The boys slept in dormitories and the lone girl had a room and bathroom to herself. There was an extensive staff, an excellent cook who also taught poisons, and instructors for everything from assassination to surveillance. The grounds were constantly patrolled by 'gamekeepers' armed with shotguns.

The Right Honourable Bethany Stockley, Beth to her friends, codename Chaton (Kitten), was bored. The class was about surveillance and the teacher was a windy old fart who went by the codename Astral. He was expounding on the principles of the quadruple tail, and she had drifted off remembering her time in India. There were only five people in her class and all the others were boys.

"Chaton," Astral said, looking at her over his half-moon glasses. "Would you be so kind as to explain how you would set up a quadruple tail on two men walking through Covent Garden in London."

"Which road will they approach the market from?" Beth said sweetly.

"Does it make a difference?"

"Yes, Sir, it does. If they are coming up from the Strand through the lanes, which are run by the Bow Street gang, it will require one man ahead, two alternating behind and the fourth on the rooftops until they come out into the market proper. Then they can adopt a more traditional one ahead, one behind and one either side formation. But having said that, in a crowded marketplace I would prefer to have a bigger team disguised as porters and buyers who could switch the tail more frequently.

If, however, the mark is approaching from St Martin's, the streets are wider which would allow one ahead, two alternating behind and one across the road."

Beth was about to continue but Astral stopped her.

"That will do nicely, thank you." There was a soft snigger behind her. The end of the class came and Astral stopped her on the way out.

"A moment please, Chaton." Only codenames were used.

"Yes, Mr Astral?" she said innocently.

"I know these classes must seem tedious to you as your esteemed father must have taught you everything, but for the sake of your less privileged colleagues, please try to at least pretend to be interested."

"Sorry, Sir. I will," she said, giving him a curtsy. Her father was the head of the Foreign Division Mobile Unit and their most senior agent. Commodore Lord Martin Stockley of Purbeck was known variously as Marty, Martin and Boss to his special operations team the Shadows, but known as M internally. As far as Beth knew he never used the code name and would only sign letters as M if they were to his boss Admiral Turner.

The next class was more fun. It was sabotage and involved a fair amount of hands-on activity. She entered the room and realised she was the last to arrive. It was noted by their instructor, Bomber, with a pointed look as he called the class to order.

"Today's subject is bridges. How to cross them without falling off." The class laughed at his joke.

"There are many types of bridges, and they all need a different methodology if you want to take them down." He uncovered a large picture on an easel.

"These are different types of arch bridge. Note the thickness of the pillars and buttresses in each type."

A second picture showed trestle bridges and a third, the latest innovation, the cantilever bridge.

"Now can anybody tell me where the common weak point is on all these arched bridges?"

Hands went up and he chose Brindle. A nondescript boy with a Newcastle accent.

"The centre of the arch, Sir. If one was to blow out the keystone the arch would lose its integrity and collapse."

"Quite right, but what is the disadvantage of that?"

Beth put her hand up.

"Chaton?"

"Easily repaired by laying timbers across the gap."

"Correct. Collapsing the top part of an arch only makes a narrow gap leaving the piers and some of the road intact. So where should you attack this bridge to destroy it?"

If you have any questions, complaints or suggestions:
Please visit my website: www.thedorsetboy.com where
you can leave a message or subscribe to the newsletter.

Or like and follow my Facebook page:
https://www.facebook.com/thedorsetboy
Or I can be found on twitter @ChristoperCTu3

Books by Christopher C Tubbs

The Dorset Boy Series.
A Talent for Trouble
The Special Operations Flotilla
Agent Provocateur
In Dangerous Company
The Tempest
Vendetta
The Trojan Horse
La Licorne
Raider
Silverthorn
Exile
Dynasty
Empire
Revolution
Burma

The Lady Bethany Series
Graduation

The Charlamagne Griffon Chronicles
Buddha's Fist
The Pharoah's Mask
Treasure of the Serpent God
The Knights Templar

And published by Lume Books

The Scarlet Fox Series
Scarlett
A Kind of Freedom
Legacy

The Decoy Ships Series
Kingfisher

See them all at:

Website: www.thedorsetboy.com
Twitter: @ChristoherCTu3
Facebook: https://www.facebook.com/thedorsetboy/
YouTube: https://youtu.be/KCBR4ITqDi4

Published in E-Book, Paperback and Audio formats
on Amazon, Audible and iTunes

.

Printed in Great Britain
by Amazon

40653404R00142